NO MAN'S LAND

No Man's Land

CAREL VAN DER MERWE

UMUZI

For Christelle, who never doubted,
and my parents,
and for Schalk and all the others

Published by Umuzi
P.O. Box 6810, Roggebaai 8012
umuzi@randomhouse.co.za
an imprint of
Random House (Pty) Ltd
Isle of Houghton
Corner Boundary Road & Carse O'Gowrie
Houghton 2198, South Africa
www.umuzi-randomhouse.co.za

Copyright © Carel van der Merwe 2007
Carel van der Merwe hereby asserts his right
to be identified as the author of this work.

All rights reserved.
No part of this book may be reproduced or transmitted in any form
or by any means, mechanical or electronic, including photocopying
and recording, or be stored in any information storage or retrieval
system, without written permission from the publisher.

First edition, first printing 2007
ISBN: 978-1-4152-0028-5

Cover design by Abdul Amien
Cover image by Sean Wilson
Design and layout by William Dicey
Set in Palatino and Courier

Printed and bound by Paarl Print
Oosterland Street, Paarl, South Africa

I look at my life and the whole thing is incomprehensible to me. I know all the reasons and all the reasons and all the reasons, and it ends up – nothing.

Arthur Miller, The Price

In every period a certain view of the world, a collective mentality, dominates the whole mass of society ... Far more than the accidents or the historical and social circumstances of a period, it derives from the distant past, from ancient beliefs, fears and anxieties which are almost unconscious ... A society's reactions to the events of the day, to the pressure upon it, to the decisions it must face, are less a matter of logic or even self-interest than the response to an unexpressed and often inexpressible compulsion arising from the collective unconscious.

Fernand Braudel, A History of Civilizations

SOUTH AFRICA

1

He senses the enmity as he wades through the crush of people outside the room where the hearing was held. Pushed from behind, he stumbles. When he looks up he sees a photographer aiming his camera. The flashlight blinds him as he raises his arm. He forces his way past, turns into a corridor, then another, and walks quickly until he reaches a fire escape door. He goes into the stairwell, stands behind the door, listens. He waits a few minutes before he walks down to his car in the parking garage of the Johannesburg Civic Centre.

It is rush hour, road rage time: overfull minibus taxis braking recklessly, cars honking in fury, pedestrians weaving through the restless metal. It begins to rain, a cheerless spring drizzle. He slides a Van Morrison CD into the compact disc player and turns up the volume; anything to blank out thought. On the M1 North the traffic is bumper to bumper. He drives numbly, his hands and legs going mechanically through the motions.

He presses the remote control for the gate as he turns into their street. He does not want to linger in the driveway: only a week ago a resident was hijacked in the next street.

Her car is not there, the house is dark. Even though he had expected as much, his stomach lurches. He unlocks the front door and disarms the beeping alarm; inside it is cold and silent. He walks down the corridor to their bedroom, the tightness in the pit of his stomach spreading to his chest. The wardrobes in their bedroom hang open, as if they have just been burgled. Her hanging space and drawers are bare.

In the living room he ignites the gas-fired fireplace. Only now does he see her wedding ring on the mantelpiece. He sits down on a sofa. His throat is hoarse, and a headache is stirring. He closes his eyes. For now he doesn't want to think about her or the hearing – for that there is sure to be more than enough time in the coming days.

On the way to work the next morning he buys *The Star* from a ragged street vendor, opens the paper at the next traffic light. The article on page four is headlined 'Student Bomber Was Army Spy'. There is a photograph too. He winces – it looks as if he's threatening the photographer, his hand raised not to conceal but to strike, his face contorted in anger, not surprise.

'Sawubona, Rose,' he greets the receptionist, a stately Zulu matron, when he walks into the lobby of DAB Securities. Usually there is some friendly banter between them, but today she looks down and fiddles with the switchboard. And in the large trading room the other dealers try their best to look busy, even though the bond market opens only in half an hour. On several desks he sees that morning's newspaper. On his keyboard is a note: from the Human Resources director.

He takes the lift to the fourth floor. After some initial throat-clearing and scribbling on a note pad, John Maxwell, a portly middle-aged Englishman with the beginnings of a double chin, gets quickly to the point. 'Paul, I'm sure you'll understand. The firm's reputation, our empowerment shareholders and the new chairman, you know what I mean?'

'Sure,' he says. Why argue? The decision has been made, probably not by John, and after yesterday's interrogation he is weary of talking. He participates uninterestedly in the well-lubricated exit process; John has done this often. So that's it, then. Five years down the drain. He had joined just after the 1994 elections, his second job after leaving university. And John has also aged since that first interview, the web of burst capillaries that spanned his nose now spreading over his cheeks.

When he is finished, John stands up and extends a damp hand. 'The firm will be generous – three months' salary instead of the statutory one month, and a very favourable recommendation letter, of course.' John walks him to the door, puts a fatherly hand on his shoulder. 'This is a minor setback, Paul, in the bigger scheme of things. You're a young chap still.'

From the averted heads in the trading room he can see that everyone already knows. While he clears his desk a fellow trader – next to whom he has worked for two years – half-heartedly suggests a drink after work. He declines, senses the relief. The farewell is awkward: a few handshakes, muted greetings, the long walk out.

The traffic flowing in from the northern suburbs is still heavy as he drives past in the opposite direction. To his surprise, a feeling of relief is mingled with the disappointment. He is free, cut loose from a life in which the years had merged seamlessly, years in which each working day had been expended watching and anticipating the changes in the yields of half a dozen government bonds.

His suburb is quiet; the only people he sees are garden boys sweeping driveways and housewives returning from the school run. Dew glints on the bleached lawns, and the air smells sooty from the anthracite fires in the townships around Johannesburg.

In the kitchen the answering machine is blinking. For a moment he is hopeful. But the tinny voice is that of Dawid, Louise's younger brother. 'Paul, Louise asked me to call. I want to arrange a time to pick up the rest of her things.'

Dawid keeps him holding – probably deliberately, he suspects. Even at high school Dawid had been a little politician, always ingratiating himself with the older boys and the teachers, and now that he is an up-and-coming partner in a large law firm he has become insufferable.

The secretary eventually puts him through. Once they get past the opening formalities he asks, 'Dawid, is Louise staying with you?'

Dawid's voice takes on a lawyerly timbre. 'Paul, it is her wish that I do not disclose her whereabouts to you. I'm sure you'll appreciate her position.'

He holds back his anger while they fix a time when Dawid can come round in the evening. He spends the rest of the day composing a letter to Louise. The phone rings half a dozen times, and he listens as the answering machine picks up: another call from his mother, several calls from journalists, two from Captain Harris, the last one from his brother in New York.

Ever the eager beaver, Dawid comes prepared with a list. They don't talk while they carry the colour television, a sofa, most of the books and compact discs, several rugs and the remainder of Louise's clothes to Dawid's borrowed bakkie. He does not argue. Let her have what she wants, let her play it out her way – they will talk when she has calmed down.

Dawid is even more overweight than he was at school and they have to rest several times so he can catch his breath. He wonders if Dawid remembers how in high school he prevented the Salvation Army boys from bullying him.

When everything is loaded into the bakkie, Dawid says in parting, 'She says you can keep the bed.'

'That's good of her.' But he softens his tone when he adds, 'Dawid, please tell her I really want to talk to her.'

11

'I don't think she's going to change her mind.'

Dawid's lips stretch in a thin smile as he slides up the bakkie's window and begins to reverse out of the driveway. 'Don't worry, I'm sure you'll be hearing from her soon.'

Some time later in the evening he orders a pizza from Mr Delivery. His stomach feels knotted and he eats only two slices. At eleven he drives to Dawid's suburb. He parks his car in the next street. The streets are deserted, but as he walks towards the house a security company van slows down next to him. After a few seconds the vehicle drives off, the patrol officers seemingly of the opinion that a neatly dressed white male must be a resident of the suburb. Careful not to touch the electric fencing, he pulls himself up and looks over Dawid's garden wall – no Mazda. He drops the letter to Louise through the mailbox and returns to his car.

Back home, he struggles to fall asleep. After seven years he misses the usual bedtime rituals: Louise taking a bath while he reads in bed, watching her comb out her long hair in the large mirror in the bedroom, later her steady breathing next to him. Her absence has marked his body: his muscles ache and he feels fragile, as if he's suffering from a severe hangover.

Outside the fence crackles from time to time as the breeze brushes the branches of a large jacaranda tree against the live wires. At two in the morning a police helicopter drones its way across the suburb, its proboscis of light feeling through the garden and illuminating the bedroom.

How quickly things fall away, he thinks. In the years since what had happened he had drifted along, blended in, tried to ignore the dangers that lay in wait in the depths below his suburban life. But the past had not died, it had only been in hibernation. And now it had tracked him down.

2

It had started innocuously: a phone call at work three months earlier, one of the dozens of phone calls he took every working day. But this time it wasn't a client or colleague but a voice he hadn't heard in a long time.

'Paul, Jim Harris here.'

In his swivel chair in the trading room he stiffened as though coming to attention. 'Captain.' A colleague on the other side of the trading desk glanced up from his desk.

'Something's come up. We need to meet.' Captain Harris had never been one to waste time on social niceties.

He knew better than to ask questions – there was sure to be a good reason, and all calls in DAB Securities' trading room were recorded in case of disputes with clients.

His hand trembled as he replaced the receiver. After all these years it was unlikely to be good news. He tried to work out when he had last seen Captain Harris. Twelve, maybe thirteen, years ago. How did he look these days? Harris had been in his mid-thirties then, so he must be about fifty. That made him now the same age that Harris had been back then. They had worked together for a year, their relationship that of superior and subordinate. And their last meeting had not been a happy one.

He left work early, arriving fifteen minutes later in Melville. He parked in a side street of gentrified zinc-roofed houses with high walls and walked to the coffee shop in the main street. Captain Harris was sitting in a corner and looked out of place amongst the housewives and students at the other tables. As he walked towards him he quickly took stock: Harris's face was fleshier, his stomach pressed against the small table, streaks of grey in his moustache. But his grip was as firm as ever. 'Hello, Paul.'

'Captain,' he replied.

Harris glanced at the neighbouring tables. 'Jim, please.'

They sat down.

'Long time, no see,' Harris said.

'Yes, Captain, it has been.' The habit was hard to break, even after all the years.

For the first few minutes they talked of family and work. After leaving Military Intelligence in 1994 Harris had moved to Johannesburg and launched a private investigation firm. According to him business was booming. Massive transformation had denuded the police of investigative skills and companies increasingly used firms such as his to investigate white-collar crime.

Only after their coffees were served did his companion lean towards him and say, 'You must be wondering?'

He nodded.

Harris lit a cigarette before continuing. 'We've got a problem.'

He nodded again, not trusting himself to say anything.

Harris took a long pull on his cigarette. 'A brigadier – you don't know him, he was at HQ – is applying for amnesty, and he is going to mention our little project in Mitchells Plain.'

So, it had arrived, the day he had feared all these years. 'Why?'

Harris sighed. 'He is applying for amnesty for something else. But to qualify he has to disclose all the projects he knew of. And, unfortunately, he was in the loop on our project. He doesn't know your name, but he is going to finger me.'

He felt a stirring of hope. 'So he doesn't know about me?'

Harris shook his head. 'It's not that simple. Obviously, I'll also have to apply now, otherwise I'll leave myself open to prosecution.'

'I see.'

'So you realise what that means?'

He didn't realise anything yet: it was as though his ability to think sequentially and logically had been paralysed, and his mind could fix on only one thought – what was he going to tell Louise?

Harris continued, 'I've already met with an advocate to represent me. His name is van Vuuren. I suggest you also use him – it will be better if we use the same guy.'

He listened as Harris took him through what they needed to do: a meeting later in the week with the advocate, the preparation of amnesty applications, cross-checking of their statements, meetings with Truth and Reconciliation Commission officials.

Over the past four years he had watched the TRC hearings on state television. To date the TRC had steered clear of the activities of the old intelligence agencies. It was rumoured that politicians on both sides had made a deal – more than a few current high-ranking ANC officials had been informers on the previous government's payroll and the political fallout if these names were exposed would be hugely damaging to the new government. But, according to Harris, the deal had changed. Pressure from the ANC rank and file required sacrificial offerings: a few lower-ranking officers in exchange for both sides ignoring those higher up.

Harris sat back in his chair. 'Don't look so worried, Paul.' He grinned. 'The TRC is a fucking circus, run by the clowns. If we stick together, we'll run rings around them.'

He did not share Harris's confidence. He had seen on television how some of the TRC advocates cross-examined the amnesty applicants.

Harris gave him a hard look. 'We'll tell them what they need to hear, that's all. We're not there to apologise or ask anyone's forgiveness. It was a war, and in war there are casualties.'

After they said their goodbyes to each other in the street, he walked back to his car. The sun, distorted by smog and dust into a shimmering fireball, slipped behind the ridge of the suburb. Everything was as usual: self-appointed parking attendants waved cars into vacant bays, a white beggar – his face chafed by outdoor life and alcohol – slumped on the pavement with an outstretched hand, music boomed out of the bars. But he had crossed a border, the border between safe anonymity and public notoriety, and now he was in no man's land.

The bed sheets are tangled around his legs. He fetches a glass of water from the kitchen, goes out on the stoep. The breeze rustles the leaves of a palm tree, the rhythmic put-put of the creepy-crawly sounding from the pool. Maybe he should have told Louise immediately. But after her miscarriage she was in no state – or so he had convinced himself – to hear more bad news. Then the TRC set a date and, a week before the hearing, he could no longer hold off telling her. Carefully he had picked his ground: Nino's, a trattoria on Jan Smuts Drive, her favourite restaurant. He sent her an email from DAB Securities; they arranged to meet at the restaurant after work.

Nino's eponymous proprietor, a busy little man with a round face and stubby fingers, had greeted him heartily in an Italian accent that he suspected was only as recent as the restaurant's décor – on his way back from the restrooms on a previous visit he had overheard Nino scolding his kitchen staff in the unmistakeable flat accent of a southern suburbs boykie. 'Hallo, my friend, where's that-a lovely wife of yours?'

Louise had not yet arrived. He chose a table in a corner, set apart from the others, and ordered a whisky. He again rehearsed his explanation, his mea culpa.

A few minutes later he saw her at the restaurant's security gate. Nino rushed over to buzz her in, kissed her on both cheeks. Louise hadn't yet seen him, and he watched her as she talked to Nino, flicking her hair back when the rotund owner helped her with her coat, a little too eagerly. Several other male diners, he noticed, were examining her discreetly.

He thought of the first time he saw her, seventeen years ago in the school quadrangle. Her hair was longer now, a tumbling mass of blonde locks that cascaded down her neck and shoulders and over her back. Nearly half his life he had known her, but now he was afraid.

Nino pointed in his direction and Louise turned, gave a small wave. She walked across the restaurant, seemingly oblivious of the eyes that followed her progress. She moved gracefully, without the self-consciousness of many tall women. He stood up and pulled out a chair for her.

Raising an eyebrow, she said, 'Eating out on a week night? What's the occasion?' Her cheeks were still glowing from the cold air outside.

'Nothing really, just felt like it,' he said, trying to hide the tension in his voice.

Nino came over and bustled around their table, expounding on the specialities of the day before pouring them complimentary sherries. After they had placed their orders Louise told him about an incident at the insurance company where she worked as a senior systems programmer. She told the story with gusto, waving her hands about. He envied the enthusiasm she had for her job. It must be the orderliness of computing that she enjoyed: the rigid rules of programming, the fixed operating routines of mainframes. And at home the invoices, bank statements and utility bills were organised in colour-coded files, compact discs arranged in alphabetical order, the wardrobes and cupboards neatly ordered. And now this, this disruption of her, their, carefully constructed life.

Only when they were halfway through their main courses did he brace himself and plunge in. 'I've got something to tell you.'

She put down her knife. 'I knew there was a reason for this.' She looked at him. 'What is it?'

She listened in silence while he rushed through his account, stumbling over the words, his tongue clumsy and heavy. Her eyes remained fixed on him, the glow in her face now drained away.

When the words had petered out, she remained silent, her face frozen. She looked down at her food and speared a chip with her fork. He could hear the hum of the conversations at other tables and the clatter of plates in the kitchen.

'Louise, it was an accident. That wasn't the plan.'

Her face flushed again, she looked at him. 'How could you have got involved in something like that? He was your friend, our friend – didn't that mean anything to you?' She paused, then spoke again, in a whisper. 'How do you live with yourself?'

He started to answer, stopped. What could he say? That you lived your life, that you tried to forget the past, that over the years it had become less real? But for some things there weren't words, or the words were wrong. 'Louise, I was twenty-two. I didn't know what I was getting myself into.'

She folded her arms across her chest. 'And you hid it from me. You had another life, a life I knew nothing about.'

'I was not allowed to talk about it, then or afterwards. We were sworn to secrecy.'

'That's very convenient, isn't it?'

'And anyway, you didn't seem to be too interested in what was going on in those years.'

'What do you mean?'

'I was in the Army for four years. What did you think I was doing? Did you ever ask me, did you ever really want to know?'

She cocked her head, looked at him sideways. 'Strange what you remember. I tried, but you didn't want to talk about it. And that was different, everyone had to go. This is something else, I don't know what.'

He took a deep breath. 'This was war too, a different part of the same war.'

'Rubbish! If it was all above board, why was it all so secret? If it hadn't been for this TRC thing you would never have told me, would you?'

He felt a surge of anger and his control slipped. 'We all have our little secrets, don't we?'

For a moment, so quick that he nearly missed it, confusion, fear maybe, flickered in her eyes. 'What do you mean?'

But he couldn't say it, not then, not ever.

She pushed her chair back, grabbed her car keys and jumped up. 'I don't know you. Who are you?'

He remained seated as she walked out of the restaurant. The other diners looked curiously at him. Nino scuttled over to the table with a concerned expression, but he waved him away. He refilled his glass of wine, sitting heavy-limbed at the table, Louise's question in his mind. You are what you are; you do what you have to do, what is expected of you. He had gone to school, played rugby, attended church, reported for his National Service, enrolled at university, found a job, married, lived in the suburbs: he was the same as everyone else. Of course he regretted what had happened, but it had happened in the line of duty, two more deaths in a country where even these days on average two people an hour died violent deaths.

He sipped his wine. His life was veering away from him. The amnesty process had taken on a life of its own; he was in the maws of an implacable machine that would first grind him up, then discard him. In six days' time his past, his life, would be exposed for all to see, to pick over, to rummage through, to sneer at. His life was going to change irrevocably, that he knew. During his and Captain Harris's meetings with Advocate van Vuuren over the past few weeks they had focused on the contents and technicalities of their amnesty applications, but of what came afterwards they did not speak.

And he still had to tell his parents. His father would understand, but of his mother he was not sure.

He goes back into the bedroom and lies down. The alarm clock shows 03:20. Once or twice in the week before the hearing he had tried to talk to Louise again, but she had rebuffed him. Not that they had seen much of each other as he and Harris had meetings every day after work with van Vuuren, meetings that lasted late into the evening. And Louise supposedly had to finish a large IT project at work, so she too had come home late every evening. He should have realised she was planning something. But she had played a good game, right up to the evening before the hearing, two nights ago.

When he had got home that night the bedroom was dark and Louise was asleep. He went into the bathroom to brush his teeth. When he came back into the room her bedside lamp was on, and she was reading a book.

She looked up at him. 'Are you ready for tomorrow?'
'As ready as I'll ever be.'
She put down her book. 'I've taken the day off at work. I'll be there.'
'Thank you.' He was relieved: it seemed he had been granted a reprieve.

He got into bed. She turned to him and put her hand on his thigh. He was surprised even though the signal was familiar. He started to speak, but she put her forefinger on his mouth.

She was in a strange mood. She thrashed against him, her eyes closed and lips parted, until he had to hold her hips to slow her down.

Afterwards they lay next to each other, their bodies cooling. When he turned to her he thought he saw her eyes glistening in the half-light.

'What's wrong?' he asked.

'Nothing.' She turned on her side, away from him. 'Let's sleep. Tomorrow's going to be a long day.'

TRUTH AND RECONCILIATION COMMISSION

AMNESTY HEARING

DATE: 13 OCTOBER 1999

NAME: PAUL JOHANNES DU TOIT

APPLICATION NO: AM2351/99 (Transcript consisting of 58 pages)

HELD AT: CIVIC CENTRE, BRAAMFONTEIN, JOHANNESBURG - (NEW MATTER)

CHAIRPERSON: This is the application involving Mr Paul Johannes du Toit, who is applying for amnesty for his role in the Mitchells Plain Community Centre bombing. For the purposes of the record, I am Judge Mphasa; my colleagues on the panel are Judge Reddy and Commissioner Barend de Wet. Can I also ask the various legal representatives to identify themselves?

MR VAN VUUREN: Mr Chairman, if it may please you and the Honourable Members of the Committee, my name is Johan van Vuuren. I'm a member of the Pretoria Bar and I appear on behalf of Mr du Toit.

MR MAUBANE: Thank you, Chairperson. I am Richard Maubane, from the Johannesburg Bar, instructed by the Legal Resource Centre in Johannesburg to appear on behalf of the families of Mr André Pretorius and Mr Ebrahim Peters.

CHAIRPERSON: Thank you. Mr du Toit, do you have an objection against taking the oath?

MR DU TOIT: No, Mr Chairman.

PAUL JOHANNES DU TOIT: (sworn states)

EXAMINATION BY MR VAN VUUREN: Thank you, Mr Chairman. Mr du Toit, you've prepared a statement which is before the panel, marked Exhibit A. Before we deal with that statement I refer you to the bundle prepared by the TRC and page 1 in particular. Is it correct that that is your amnesty application, completed in your handwriting and signed by yourself, and do you confirm the evidence that I will be leading shortly?

MR DU TOIT: Yes.

MR VAN VUUREN: Thank you. I then refer you to Exhibit A. You set out in Exhibit A your personal background and your family situation. You were born in the Thabazimbi district in 1964, and your family moved to Pretoria when you were nine years old. You then deal with your family situation and some of the incidents that formulated or influenced your thinking in later years. Could you start off by reading paragraphs 2, 3, 4 and 5 into the record.

MR DU TOIT: 'We moved to Pretoria when my father was elected as the National Party Member of Parliament for the Pretoria East area. At home and school we often discussed historical and political issues. I learnt about the Afrikaners' struggle for independence, how the Voortrekkers embarked on the Great Trek out of the Cape Colony in 1838 to escape British rule, and how they subsequently established their own independent republics in the Transvaal and Orange Free State. I also learnt how, in 1899, Great Britain attacked and conquered the Boer republics, and of the deaths in British concentration camps of twenty-six thousand Boer women and children, approximately ten per cent of the Afrikaner population of that time.

'My paternal great-grandfather fought in the war against the British. He was captured and imprisoned for two years in Ceylon. His daughter, my grandmother, survived the deaths of her mother and younger brother in a concentration camp. Afterwards she, and those of her generation, worked tirelessly to restore power to the Afrikaner nation. From childhood it was instilled in me that, having regained our country, we had to defend it at all costs, so as to never again end up in a similar situation.

'I understood that the rationale for apartheid, or the separate development of the races, was that each people who defined themselves as a nation had a right to their own land and independence, free from the domination of any other nation. I accepted this rationale, namely that the white people of South Africa were a separate nation to the various Black tribes such as the Xhosas, Zulus, Sothos and so on. They had their own countries, the homelands, just like South Africa was our country.

'At my high school in Pretoria all boys had to participate in weekly drilling sessions in military uniforms. I was a member of the school cadet team, and in Matric I captained the school shooting team. During that time, following the Soweto riots in 1976, there was an increase in political unrest. We were told that this was due to Communist agitation of our Black population, instigated by the Soviet Union. The Communist goal was the takeover of South Africa, as its mineral resources and the sea route around the Cape were of strategic importance to the West. I was under the impression that most Black people in South Africa were content. I thought from everything I read and heard that the ANC represented an insignificant part of the Black population of South Africa, and that it was the puppet of the Soviet Union.'

MR VAN VUUREN: You then list in paragraph 6 a number of incidents that were central to your life experience. Are there any of those that you would like to elaborate on? You may consult your notes.

MR DU TOIT: Yes. In 1981, in my Matric year, my uncle and cousin were killed by a landmine on a road near their farm in the Northern Transvaal. The ANC claimed responsibility for this incident. I was very upset by this. I decided to do my two years' National Service before going to university. I wanted to fight the enemy.

MR VAN VUUREN: Thank you. Let's then move on to your military training and experiences. Can you please read paragraphs 7 and 8 of your application?

MR DU TOIT: 'I was called up to the South African Navy, and did my basic training at Saldanha Bay from January to March 1982. At the end of my basic training I was selected for Special Forces training. I completed my Operator's training a year later, in March 1983. I also signed up for three years' Permanent Force service in addition to my two years' National Service, as this was a requirement for joining Special Forces. From 1983 to 1985 I was deployed on operations in Angola. During this time we encountered not only SWAPO insurgents, but also various Soviet and Warsaw Pact forces, including Russians, Ukrainians, East Germans and Cubans. This further convinced me that South Africa faced a grave threat from Communists.

'In September 1985 I was wounded during an operation and I had several operations on my right knee at 2 Military Hospital in Cape Town. During this time, while I was undergoing rehabilitation treatment, I was advised that I would not be able to take part in Special Forces operations again.'

MR VAN VUUREN: Why was this?

MR DU TOIT: Because of the injury to my knee. Although I could walk okay, my knee couldn't take much weight.

MR VAN VUUREN: And why was that a problem?

MR DU TOIT: Because of the way Special Forces operated. We acted in small units with little support. We had to gather strategic and tactical intelligence about the enemy behind his lines. During long-distance operations in Angola we had to carry kit that could weigh up to seventy, eighty kilograms. So, when we were spotted by enemy forces during operations, we sometimes had to evade capture on foot over hundreds of kilometres. Obviously my injury made me unfit for that kind of thing.

MR VAN VUUREN: Is it correct to say that during your time in the Defence Force you encountered the then enemy on many occasions?

MR DU TOIT: That's correct.

MR VAN VUUREN: And during these contacts there was fire?

MR DU TOIT: That's correct.

MR VAN VUUREN: In other words, there was shooting at each other, people were killed?

MR DU TOIT: Yes.

3

The morning after Dawid's visit he steels himself and phones Louise at work. She resigned a week earlier, a secretary informs him. And no, they don't have her new contact details. When he puts down the phone his heart is hammering. She had resigned even before his hearing; her flight had been carefully planned, he realises. Her parents live in a coastal retirement village, but she loathes her father so it's unlikely that she'll be there, and other than Dawid she has no close family.

He is supposed to attend Captain Harris's hearing, but he can't face returning to that room. Instead he systematically phones their mutual acquaintances and her friends. But nobody knows where she is, or if they do, they are not telling. He has become a pariah, that much is clear. No one talks or asks about his hearing, and he can sense that his calls aren't welcome. It is the new South Africa and he is an unwelcome reminder of the past, a past most whites want to forget or ignore. Not only has he killed, he has killed one of their own. His crimes had been for the nation, he had argued at the hearing. But that nation is in denial: the past is the past, things happened that they weren't aware of, it is now time to move on. It is now the time of the Rainbow Nation, a nation born out of a political miracle, a virgin birth.

On the evening news there is a brief insert about Captain Harris's hearing. The female journalist in front of the Civic Centre describes him as a recalcitrant applicant whom the TRC advocate had struggled to pin down.

In the ensuing days he seldom leaves the house. After the newspaper articles and his brief appearance on the television news he feels exposed and vulnerable in public places. He sometimes detects furtive glances in his direction; once in a shop he catches a flash of recognition in a stranger's eyes. The smell of food nauseates him and he eats little. One evening he tries, and fails, to get drunk – it seems he has even lost his taste for alcohol. The top of his ribcage aches and the thin layer of flesh over his breastbone feels bruised, as if he has been dealt a staggering blow to the chest. In the evenings he watches television on a small portable set until his eyes are numb; afterwards he struggles to fall asleep. Sometimes he wakes up during the night with a racing heart and drenched in sweat;

the next day he can't remember the dreams. He lies in bed until eleven or twelve in the mornings, drifting in and out of sleep.

One morning he doesn't shave. After that he stops altogether. In the sink the plates and cups pile up. During the day he wanders through the house. There is little to show that she once lived here: some wilting flowers in a vase, decaying yogurt in the fridge, a T-shirt that ended up in his drawer. He is overwhelmed by a paralysing lethargy; he should be doing something, planning his future, but a continuous low-grade headache makes coherent thought difficult. Time, which he had carefully meted out and cordoned off before, is now an abundant commodity. One evening he realises he hasn't spoken to anyone in two days.

He lives in anticipation. When the phone rings he waits anxiously next to the answering machine, willing it to pick up faster. A couple of older friends, Captain Harris, his mother every day – never Louise. He doesn't return the calls. The sporadic ringing of the doorbell he ignores; she has her own key.

Her decision to leave him must have been made during the hearing, an impulsive reaction to Advocate Maubane's allegations, he sometimes thinks. And surely a decision made on the spur of the moment could be rescinded, could be appealed against. But at other times he is assailed by doubt. He thinks of what happened the night before the hearing: Louise gripping him with an intensity that went beyond passion; a kind of immolation, a kind of leave-taking? But she had resigned a week before the hearing – why then had she come to the hearing? Out of pity, a feigned display of support? Every question gives rise to another, a repetitive sequence that without respite loops through his mind, sending him from room to room and out into the garden, then back in again.

He also does not know at what stage of the hearing she left. But most likely it had been after Brad Friedman's affidavit was read out. He does not know because during the hearing he had avoided looking at the public gallery, as there sat the Peters family and Leon, André's older brother. Beforehand he had seen Leon come into the room; he had walked towards him, hand outstretched, but Leon had turned away. Then a TRC official had pointed out the Peters family. Mrs Peters, an elderly coloured woman, was already seated, her handbag clasped on her lap. She was flanked by two younger women, who both looked away when they saw him watching them. But Mrs Peters had looked at him with what had seemed like – and he struggles to articulate it – sympathy, a look that he could not bear.

His mother keeps on phoning, her messages becoming increasingly insistent. Eventually, three weeks after the hearing, he phones back, agrees to visit.

On the day he wakes only at noon; he had intended to set out earlier but had fallen asleep only as dawn was breaking. With a sinking feeling he visualises the journey: the busy highway between Johannesburg and Pretoria, after that the long stretch to Warmbaths, then a dirt road to the farm in the heart of the Waterberg. The drive will be tedious, the visit even more so.

It takes him twenty minutes to shave off his week-old beard. He examines himself in the mirror. His skin is yellowish and there are dark bruises under his eyes; he looks like someone in the throes of a debilitating illness. He considers phoning with an excuse. But that would only postpone the trip, and his mother might even take it into her head to drive to Johannesburg. Better to go and get it over with. But he dawdles and it is mid-afternoon by the time he leaves the house.

Forty kilometres past Pretoria he nods off, waking up with a start when the BMW's tyres hit the gravel shoulder of the road. He skids to a stop in a cloud of dust. After a minute or so he drives on, his foot shaking on the accelerator. But even the shock of the near-accident can't keep his lassitude at bay, and from time to time he has to wet his eyelids with saliva to keep them from giving in to sleep.

Scores of minibuses slow down the Friday afternoon traffic and it is after seven when he turns into the farm. He winds down his window. The terrain of his youth. The evening air smells of bush and dust and woodsmoke. A herd of young impala males prances across the road just as he rounds the last bend before the thatch-roofed house. As he drives into the farmstead his mother comes down the steps to meet him. His father watches impassively from the stoep.

She embraces him, then looks him up and down. Her examination grates on him. His father comes down the steps and shakes his hand, his grip unexpectedly soft. He takes his bag through to his old room, where he slept for the first nine years of his life. His mother has been redecorating: the bed and curtains are new, as is the colour of the walls. The traces of the past are few – an antique yellowwood wardrobe, a carved African mask on the wall.

Supper has been laid out on the stoep. Before they eat his father recites a prayer, his sonorous voice rising and falling, its cadences honed by his many years as a church elder and politician. He examines his parents while their eyes are closed. They have grown old, older than he remembers. His mother's hair is thinning, the skin under his father's chin is slack.

His mother has prepared his favourites: roast lamb, sweet potatoes, pumpkin, rice and gravy. But he picks at his food, the sight of the laden table oppressive. The insect light on the wall buzzes sporadically as moths flutter out of the darkness and annihilate themselves. There is the old wariness between his father and himself and the conversation is slow. His mother does her best: the recent rains, the illness of one of his childhood acquaintances, local comings and goings. His father looks down at his plate while he eats. Only when she mentions that Pieter, his brother, has been promoted at the New York advertising agency he works for does his father briefly look up and give a curt snort.

They are drinking coffee when his mother hesitantly asks, 'And Louise, have you heard from her?'

He shakes his head, his throat tightening.

His father folds his hands together. 'Maybe it's for the better. I mean, if she can't stand by your side at a time like this.'

He feels the blood rush to his face but bites back a retort.

After dinner his parents go to bed. He stays behind on the stoep to smoke a cigarette. Down in the valley the trees are silvery blue under a full moon, and somewhere in the distance a jackal howls. Near the dam impala grunt. Louise never really liked coming here, he thinks, she was an urbanite, unaccustomed to the slower rhythms and small discomforts of a farm.

He hears a soft footfall behind him. It is his mother in her nightdress, her grey hair loose; a grandmother without grandchildren. She sits down in a chair opposite him. He feels himself tense: she has come to talk.

'It's a nice evening,' she says.

He nods.

She reaches across the table and puts her hand on his. 'My child.'

He pulls his hand away. 'Ma, I'm fine, okay,' he says, in a harsher tone than he intended.

She blinks. 'Paul, this too shall pass. Remember, God never tests us for no reason.'

As usual her cloying religiosity irks him. To his mother everything that happened was part of God's master plan, a plan that mere mortals could not comprehend. His own childhood faith, never strong, had petered out a long time ago.

She continues, 'Have you gone to see his mother or the other man's family?'

He shakes his head. Even now she can't say André's name, he realises. He remembers André's brother turning away, Mrs Peters' unfathomable look. He had thought about going to see them before the hearing, but Advocate van Vuuren had dissuaded him: better not, it could give rise to complications. But he remembers also that the legal advice had come as a relief. And what purpose would be served by going now? He has confessed; nothing he says can undo what happened. And what about his cousin and uncle, whose bodies, according to the police report, had been so badly burnt in their bakkie that they had fused together in a macabre embrace? No one from the other side had confessed to planting that mine, nor had anyone asked Tannie Marie for forgiveness.

His mother is looking at him, waiting. 'Ma, please. Not now.'

For a few seconds only the repetitive *chirr-chirr* of a nightjar disturbs the silence. Then she speaks again. 'Paul, you can't carry this alone. God forgives us, but you first have to make your peace here on earth.'

He stands up. 'Ma, I'm tired, I'm going to sleep.' He stubs out his cigarette and walks into the house, leaving her in the darkness.

The next morning his father drives him around the farm. His father points out the additions – funded by a generous parliamentary pension – that he has recently made to the farm: six rondavels to accommodate hunters, a slaughterhouse where game can be skinned and cut up, a new dam, electric fencing. His parents had moved back to the farm after his father lost his parliamentary seat five years ago. Then it had still been a cattle farm, managed by a neighbouring farmer on his father's behalf. But in the last few years the livestock industry had become an unprofitable one. The upsurge in tourism after the 1994 elections had brought with it an influx of foreign trophy hunters into the country and, a year ago, his father had decided to discontinue cattle farming and to stock the farm with game.

The bush is dense from the early rainfall and they see little of the various antelope species, rhino, buffalo and giraffe that his father has settled on the farm. At noon they stop on a koppie overlooking the valley and open the hamper that his mother has prepared. They take their sandwiches and cans of beer and sit down on a large boulder. In a break in the bush in the valley a herd of giraffe is moving slowly through a copse and methodically stripping the leaves from the trees, their long necks gracefully bending and unbending. He and his father eat in silence; they have exhausted everything there is to say about the farm.

Their relationship is that of polite acquaintances, he thinks. When they lived in Pretoria his father had to be in Cape Town for six months of the year to attend Parliament; during the other six months there were constituency speeches to be made and party officials to be met. And when his father was at home, Pieter and he had to listen to interminable political monologues, captive guinea pigs for a politician who never tired of hearing his own voice. But now his father is silent at last, his old profundities and rhetoric redundant.

Eventually his father turns to him. 'Look, I'm sure you know that your mother and I are behind you,' he says. 'And of course we know that what happened was an accident. After all, you were just following instructions, doing your job.' He sips from his can. 'But I must say, I didn't know that the Army had a programme like that in the eighties.'

He is taken aback. This is the first time his father has talked about what came out at the hearing. 'Ja, it seems a lot of people didn't know what was going on,' he says.

His father frowns.

He considers elaborating on his statement, then decides not to. What's the point? The politicians who had sent them to do their dirty work in the neigbouring countries and the black townships now denied knowing the details of what happened. And the generals blamed their subordinates for misinterpreting their orders. Secure with their guaranteed government pensions and coastal retirement houses and game farms, they had adapted quite well to the new South Africa. But his generation, the generation that had listened and believed, had been cut adrift and left to atone for the sins of their fathers.

They finish their sandwiches in silence. Afterwards his father wants to drive over to the other side of the farm to look for an injured giraffe. He tells his father that he is going to walk home, he wants to exercise his knee.

'It's a long walk, are you sure?' his father asks as he climbs into the Land Rover.

'Yes.'

'Then take my .303. There's an old leopard about; one of the workers spotted him near their compound the other night.'

He does not want to be lumbered with a rifle, and leopards seldom move about in daylight. 'No thanks.'

'Take it. Please.'

He looks up, surprised, and takes the rifle. He watches the Land Rover drive away, a cloud of dust marking its progress. When it disappears from view he starts walking. It is hot and soon his shirt is damp. After a while he adopts the army shuffle that covers maximum ground with minimum exertion. Other than a few birds, he doesn't see any wild life; in this heat the animals will all be resting in the shade. But their spoor and middens are everywhere: kudu, gemsbok, rooibok, giraffe, waterbuck. And he sees also the slither marks of black mambas in the dust. He is wearing only shorts and veldskoens, so he stays on the dirt road. At first his knee aches, but gradually the throbbing recedes. It feels good to be in the bush, to inhale the scents. As always, at the back of his mind is Louise, but for once the volume is muted.

It is late in the afternoon when he reaches the dam, a kilometre from the farmstead. He finds a comfortable spot on the bank from where to watch the sun set. Flocks of birds dive and swirl over the water, their last flurry of flight before darkness falls. A mournful cry drifts across the water and echoes across the valley. It is the call of a fish eagle, a bird that mates for life, he remembers, and which, when its mate dies, never takes another. The sun slips behind the Kransberge, like an inflamed eye shutting.

It is dark when he walks into the farmstead. They sit down for an early supper. For long stretches no one talks. He can see that his mother senses the uneasiness between him and his father. Afterwards he pleads exhaustion and goes to his room.

His father is out on the farm somewhere, his mother tells him when he comes into the kitchen on Sunday morning. He makes a quick decision. He has a lunch date with friends, he says, he has to get going. She protests, but he is firm. Thirty minutes later he drives away from the farmstead, his mother receding in the rear-view mirror. On the back seat is a cane basket filled with biltong, droëwors and rusks.

He briefly allows himself to hope just before he turns into the driveway, but everything is as he left it two days ago: the drawn curtains, the overgrown garden, the two empty parking bays. That night he again sleeps on her side of the bed. But her scent has faded from the pillows.

4

The visit to the farm seems to mark a turning point of sorts. On Monday morning he wakes earlier than usual. The bedroom is bathed in sunlight. Outside he sees a hadeda descending onto the lawn with a raucous caw-caw. Something feels different; then he realises that for the first time in a month he hasn't got a headache. As usual his first thoughts are of Louise, but this time he feels angry. She left without explanation, without even giving him another chance to put his case. And by leaving so abruptly she has made him a figure of pity and scorn, the humiliated husband. But they are still married; he must be patient, she is sure to surface eventually. For now he must grit his teeth, press on.

After breakfast he wades through the pile of unopened mail: overdue rent and car payments, utility bills, bank statements. DAB Securities has deposited his termination money into his bank account, less than he had expected. Unfortunately it is correct, he realises after a few calculations. The amount has been based on his basic salary, but his annual bonuses had always exceeded that. And the bonuses had been frittered away on intangibles – they had never skimped on holidays and entertainment. He will have to do something about money, there's not much to show for the years of work.

The placement consultant at the first personnel agency he phones is enthusiastic to begin with, but her voice cools when he gives her more information. She'll put his name on their database, the market is difficult right now. No, he doesn't have to come in to discuss his CV, a letter will do just fine; she'll be in contact if anything comes up. He phones three other agencies. After some questioning the first two inform him that they are not taking on any new clients, but at the third he gets an appointment for the next morning.

The agency is in a new business park in Sandton. A lawn sprinkler scythes water across his windscreen as he parks in front of the building and sprays the back of his shirt when he gets out. He puts on his jacket and tries to dodge the water. It feels strange to once again wear a suit; earlier that morning he had struggled for ten minutes to tie a Windsor knot.

He is early. The receptionist to whom he announces himself in the marble lobby motions him to a leather couch. He feels her eyes on him as he picks up *Business Day* – does she recognise him?

'Paul du Toit?'

He looks up at a pretty raven-haired woman – mid to late twenties, sleek in a dark trouser suit and silk blouse buttoned at the neck – smiling at him, her hand extended. He follows her down a corridor and into a glass-fronted meeting room. They sit down at a round table. She fills in a questionnaire while interviewing him. When she has completed the form she shuts her folder with a brisk snap. For a few moments they look at each other in silence. He folds and unfolds his hands under the table.

She shifts in her chair as if she's uncomfortable, nibbles on the cap of her pen before she says, 'The market's a bit tight at the moment, but I'll see what I can do.'

He puts his hands on the table. 'What about the international players? I hear Merrills and UBS want to increase their trading capacity.'

She looks down, then at him. 'Paul, I have to be honest. Everyone is going to want to know why you left DAB.'

He hides his disappointment, holds her eyes. 'And?'

'And, unfortunately, that is going to make it very difficult to place you,' she says apologetically.

'Why?'

He feels a twinge of sympathy for her. He knows what she's going to say and these days people have to tread carefully through this particular minefield. But he wants her to tell him; he wants it spelt out.

She coughs discreetly. 'With all the changes … companies are very sensitive about their reputations and who they employ, particularly if they get any business from the government or the public sector.'

Afterwards she walks him back to the lobby where they shake hands. 'Good luck,' she says, and gives his hand a light squeeze.

He widens his job search. Most of the advertisements in the financial magazines are for affirmative action candidates. When he follows up those that aren't, he is invariably asked at some stage whether he is a member of a previously disadvantaged community. No, he answers. But he is tempted to add: I am, however, a member of a currently disadvantaged community, a white Afrikaner male, a species on which it's now open season. Royal game in one generation, a pestilence in the next. But how do you argue against the irony – the justice even – of history?

The days pass slowly. In the mornings he scans the appointment pages of the newspapers and writes job applications; in the afternoons he walks around Emmarentia Dam, joining the pensioners exercising their dogs; in the evenings he watches television.

He avoids his friends: he doesn't want sympathy and questions. In any case, most of his friendships nowadays are work-related. Friendships that are guarded and do not allow the casual confidences of youth, that have been constructed on shifting ground. Even in older friendships there are undercurrents of envy and rivalry. Salaries, jobs, houses and cars are surreptitiously compared, weighed, resented. And no doubt some of the expressions of sympathy will be tinged with Schadenfreude. The messages soon fizzle out; eventually they stop altogether.

Captain Harris, who has left several messages in the past weeks, phones again. This time he takes the call. He concocts an excuse: he was up at the farm, helping his father. Harris doesn't sound convinced. He wants them to meet with Advocate van Vuuren as soon as possible to get clarity on the way forward.

The meeting is at van Vuuren's house in Hyde Park – two days later and in the evening because of van Vuuren's tight schedule. A security guard opens the ten-foot-high gate. He drives down a winding driveway, past an Olympic-sized swimming pool and a tennis court on which two teenage girls are hitting balls at each other under floodlights, and parks outside the large double-storey house with a thatch roof. Captain Harris's Mercedes is parked next to a Range Rover and a Porsche. The new South Africa, it seems, has been profitable for some.

A black maid lets him into the house and leads him down a long hallway and through the large dining room. Harris and van Vuuren are seated on the patio, half-full glasses of beer in front of them on the glass table. The meeting appears to have started without him.

Van Vuuren, a dapper middle-aged man with a quick smile and restless eyes, offers him a drink, exchanges a few pleasantries, then quickly gets to the point. 'Paul, I've just been telling Jim here that the TRC should reach a decision on your application by no later than March next year.'

Another four months of uncertainty. 'And what do you think?' he asks.

Van Vuuren's eyes flicker between him and Harris. 'About your chances?'

He nods.

Van Vuuren puts his hands together as if preparing to pray. 'It's difficult to say with these things – after all, this whole TRC thing is new ground for all of us. But I would say good, quite good.'

Harris asks, 'What does that mean? Fifty-fifty, sixty-forty, ninety-ten?'

The advocate massages his temples with his fingers. 'Look, the law is not an exact science. But I would say better than even, definitely. In a court of law I would be even more sure, but the TRC is not a court of law. This matter that came up at the end, you know, this suspicion that was planted about Paul, that muddied the waters a bit.'

Harris says, 'But that's bullshit, man. There's no proof that that played any role, and I for one would have known if it had.'

The advocate grimaces. 'As I said, the TRC is not a court of law – it is up to an applicant to prove that he committed his act for political reasons. And remember, even if amnesty is refused it has no legal consequences. The onus remains on the State to make a case in a proper court of law.'

The maid has come back to the patio. 'Master, there is someone on the phone.' Van Vuuren excuses himself and goes into the house.

Harris mutters, 'Bloody lawyers. You can never get a straight answer out of them.' He lights a cigarette. 'And you, how are you?'

'So-so. Lost my job.'

Harris nods. 'Ja, it's not easy.' He punches him on the shoulder. 'But don't worry so much.'

Van Vuuren returns, clears his throat. 'Sorry guys, I've got something of a crisis on my hands – client wants an urgent interdict. I have to get back to the office. But I think we're done here anyway, not so?' He escorts them out, visibly eager to be rid of them. The Defence Force retained him to represent them before and at the hearing only. Pro bono work is clearly not part of his services.

As the gate closes behind them, Harris brakes in front of him and gets out of his car. He approaches and asks, 'Want to have a beer somewhere?'

'Sorry, can't. Have to get home.'

'Sure, sure, I understand.' Harris hesitates, seeming to consider something, then says, 'Have you found a new job?'

'No, still looking.'

'What about coming to work for me, or rather, with me? I can always use another hand.' He listens as Harris explains. Can he really be serious? The two of them, together again!

'So, what do you think?' Harris says in conclusion.

He weighs up several answers before replying. 'Interesting idea. Thanks for the offer.'

'And?'

'Can I think about it?'

Harris frowns. 'Sure. But don't take too long.'

When he gets home there is a message on the answering machine: Dawid wants to talk about Louise, would he please phone him the next morning? He replays the message a few times, analyses the inflections of her brother's words. Dawid's voice is neutral, friendly even. He considers phoning Dawid at home and decides against it; it won't do to look too eager.

He pours himself a large whisky, drinks it quickly, pours another. He goes outside and paces up and down in the garden. More than a month has passed, enough time for her to reflect, to reconsider. And she's clever to choose Dawid as the intermediary: using a friend would have risked gossip. There are sure to be conditions – initial meetings, heart-to-heart talks, a trial period maybe.

He phones Dawid's office at five past eight in the morning. Dawid is not in yet, but his secretary has been expecting the call. Dawid wants to meet that afternoon at three, if possible. It will be the three of them at the meeting, she says in response to his question.

He considers what to wear, eventually decides to dress casually – after all, it is not a business meeting. He irons a pair of chinos and a long-sleeved shirt, shaves meticulously. At half-past two he drives to the law firm in Parktown North. The sun glares off the mirrored building.

The prim receptionist examines him with an air of disapproval, and tells him to wait in the lobby, furnished with what look to be antique pieces. Time passes slowly. Louise is probably already ensconsed in Dawid's office. The hushed silence is disturbed only by lawyers with serious expressions fetching their clients from time to time and the muffled buzzing of the switchboard.

Twenty minutes later he gets up and again walks over to the receptionist. Mr Smit is aware that he has arrived, she assures him. Dawid is deliberately keeping him waiting, he realises. What the origin of Dawid's antipathy towards him is, he does not know. At school he had never taken much notice of Dawid: he was Louise's younger brother, an overweight and bullied boy who was useless at all sports, a peripheral figure. And Dawid had sat out his National Service in an office job in the Air Force personnel department in Pretoria, medically unfit for active duty. But those days are long gone. Dawid has somehow transformed into a self-confident and arrogant contract lawyer, that most irritating specimen of corporate parasite.

Another ten minutes pass before Dawid's secretary fetches him. She escorts him down several corridors and into a boardroom. Dawid, his thinning hair jelled back, sits at the head of a gleaming mahogany table, flanked by a flint-faced woman, leather folders and documents opened in front of them. Louise is not there. His stomach tightens.

Dawid gets up, teeth flashing and hand outstretched. 'Paul, thanks for coming on such short notice. Sorry about keeping you waiting.' He shrugs his shoulders. 'Clients, what can you do? No rest for the wicked.'

The woman regards him coolly. 'Deborah Richardson, from our Family Law department,' Dawid says. 'She's going to be sitting in – hope you don't mind.'

She nods in his direction. 'Mr du Toit.'

In his mouth he tastes acid; he has walked into an ambush.

They sit down. Dawid opens a folder, crosses his arms over his chest.

'Paul, we don't want to waste your time, so I'm not going to beat around the bush. I'm sure you know what this meeting's about?'

He shakes his head.

Dawid's eyebrows lift in seeming amazement, but his eyes betray him. 'But I thought I told you that you would be hearing from her.'

For a moment he considers reaching over the table and punching his smug mouth. Dawid's smile fades and he lifts his hand. 'Relax, relax.' He turns to his colleague. 'Deborah, perhaps you would like to take it from here?'

She picks up a document, clears her throat. 'Mr du Toit, I am representing Mrs du Toit. I am ...'

'Where is she?' he says.

Dawid says, 'Paul, that's not relevant at this juncture.'

'Where is she?'

The female lawyer continues, unruffled: 'Mr du Toit, Mrs du Toit is seeking a divorce from you. Her current whereabouts are not at issue here.'

He pushes back his chair and gets up. 'Then I see no reason for me to be here.'

Dawid struggles to his feet, his face reddening. 'This is unacceptable. You can't just walk out.'

He steps towards Dawid. 'Really?'

'Mr du Toit, please,' Deborah intervenes. 'We were hoping to settle this matter amicably. She wants nothing from you, there are no children, few assets; it is a simple matter.' She holds out the document to him. 'I have taken the liberty of preparing a settlement agreement. Take it away, read it at your leisure. If you sign it, this matter can be handled expeditiously.'

He doesn't take the proffered document. 'And if I don't?'

She frowns. 'Mr du Toit, my client is of the opinion that your marriage has irretrievably broken down, and she has left you. This, together with what came out at your TRC hearing, constitutes overwhelming grounds for a divorce, and no court will refuse her application. At best you are only delaying the process.'

'Then so be it.'

As he walks out Dawid says, 'You'll be hearing from us.'

5

He leaves at six that same evening. It is a thirteen-hour drive to Sedgefield, the coastal town where her parents live. In the past weeks he had phoned twice, and twice Louise's father had cut him short. This time he will go and prostrate himself, if that is what is required of him.

During the first few hours on the road a jumble of thoughts assail him: the hearing, Mrs Peters' face, Louise's expression when he told her. He thinks about the meeting earlier in the day with Dawid and is filled with dread. Once again a process has been started over which he has no control.

At ten he refuels at an all-night service station outside Bloemfontein. Advertising banners flutter in the wind that gusts out of the darkness. In the distance the city's lights illuminate low, fleeting clouds.

After Bloemfontein the dual carriageway narrows to a single lane. The night seems to push back against the beams of the car's headlamps, diffusing the light to the sides of the road and the surrounding veld. The rush of the tyres on the tarmac, the road unfolding in front of him, the great emptiness, all these gradually calm his thoughts.

It is a clear night and a glittering white river flows across the firmament. He races through the iron landscape of the Karoo, sometimes driving twenty or thirty kilometres before he encounters another car. Now and then he sees the faint lights of a solitary farmhouse in the distance, like those of a ship ploughing its way through a dark sea. He feels adrift in the vastness, freed from himself and the events of the last few months. Again he gets the feeling that some places in the country evoke in him, a feeling that he knows this landscape intimately, that in a previous life he inhabited this land. Old land, he thinks. Karoo was the Hottentot word for 'thirst land'. But the Hottentots are no more, obliterated by the settlers' diseases and alcohol.

At three in morning he reaches Graaff-Reinet – the seat of a short-lived late-eighteenth-century Boer republic, he remembers from a long past school history lesson. The wide main road of the town is deserted. But after a couple of blocks a feral-looking dog lopes out of a side street and trots alongside the car. At a petrol station he wakes two attendants sleeping in a kiosk, refuels, buys cigarettes. When he drives out of the garage he sees the dog across the road, its eyes glinting red in the car's headlights.

The sun is rising over the Indian Ocean as he descends the Outeniqua pass. At Wilderness the wind is whipping foam from the wavetops, and the air flowing through the vents of the car smells of damp and salt. Somewhere near here, he recalls, lives the surprisingly small man with the dour face and black Homburg who had presided over one of their medal parades and who, later, had refused to appear before the TRC.

Ten minutes later he pulls into a service station a few kilometres from her parents' retirement village. It is seven o'clock, too early to visit. He washes his face and shaves in the restroom. Unusually for him these days, he is hungry and walks over to the restaurant. While he waits for his breakfast he looks out over the national road and a lake to the grey mountains etched on the horizon.

Familiar territory. Not far from here is the coastal resort where his father had rented a cottage during the summer school holidays. And where, a few days before he had to report for National Service, Louise and he had walked along the beach until the lights of the resort were far behind them. She had spread a towel and they had undressed in the moonlight.

Afterwards they lay intertwined on the towel, their feet touching the cool sand, Louise's head in the crook of his arm, enveloped by the deep booming of the sea and the scent of fynbos.

'You'll write?' he asked her again.

She lifted her head and kissed him on the mouth. 'Every week.'

'Anyway, Saldanha Bay is only a couple of hours from Stellenbosch University. And after eight weeks we'll get our first weekend pass,' he continued.

She smiled. 'Coming to check on me, are you?'

Those were the last uncomplicated days, he thinks, as the waitress serves him. Everything had still seemed straightforward then: Louise was his, the cause was clear, the future was unmade. And so you drift through life, oblivious of where the stream takes you.

After breakfast he drives to the retirement village, a gated community of trim gardens and one-storey houses with steep thatched roofs and whitewashed walls. Oom Rudolf opens the door, his smile fading away when he sees who it is. It is Tannie Rina who invites him in.

He waits in the sitting room while she makes coffee. He hears their voices rise and fall in the kitchen, but he can't make out what they are saying. When they come back into the sitting room Tannie Rina is carrying a large silver tray. She pours coffee and offers him a rusk.

Louise's parents sit stiffly next to each other on a heavy ball and claw mahogany sofa which he remembers from their Pretoria house. Outside he hears a lawnmower choke, elsewhere the wail of a car alarm. Oom Rudolf nods – it seems he may begin with his petition. While he talks they eye him warily from behind their coffee cups. Mother and daughter have the same eyes: large and grey-green, like a cat's, eyes that had burned into his back during the hearing.

When he finishes Louise's mother looks at her husband. Oom Rudolf's eyes blink behind his thick glasses and he shakes his head. She delicately puts her cup and saucer on the side table next to her. 'Paul, we don't have much contact with her, only a letter or phone call every now and then.' She takes Oom Rudolf's hand. 'I'm sorry, I know you came a long way, but she doesn't want you to know where she is.'

Her father walks him to his car. Through a gap in the curtains he glimpses Tannie Rina's face. When they shake hands her father's polite façade slips for a moment and he says brusquely, 'Forget about her. She wants nothing more to do with you.'

Twenty minutes from Johannesburg the headache starts, unshackled by a night and a day on the road. He immediately knows that it is going to be a bad one. The headaches are familiar enemies. Sometimes it is a dull throb in his frontal lobes that can be pacified with three or four aspirins; worse are the sharp, stabbing pains in his temporal lobes – only intensive and constant massaging of his temples gives some relief. The most severe is the one whose early probing he now detects, a pain so intense that his whole brain seems to be inflamed.

He arrives home just in time: his eyeballs are beginning to ache, and the vice around his head has tightened. From the fridge he takes the water bottle, draws the curtains and unplugs the telephone, then gets into bed.

That night and the next day he is immobilised. The headache ebbs and flows, back and forth between a sharp throbbing and an all-enveloping mist of pain, when even the slightest movement of his head sends bright flashes across his vision. He can't sleep, but neither can he get up; his world has contracted to a bed.

Sometime during the next night he falls asleep. When he wakes in the morning the pain has subsided to a dull pulse. He is hungry, and the fridge is bare.

He drives out to a large shopping centre on the outskirts of the northern suburbs, a faux-Tuscan mega-mall squatting on a hill that ripples from afar in the November heat. Around the terracotta-coloured buildings cars are parked in small clusters, as if huddling together for safety in the vast open-air parking lot. There are shops closer to home, but there he risks running into someone he knows.

A gust of cold air streams over him as he goes into the mall, the automatic doors whispering to a close behind him. Coming out of the morning glare it takes his eyes a few seconds to adjust to the dim lighting. In the entertainment area the entrance to a multiplex cinema is directly ahead, on his left various fast food franchises and branded restaurants, on his right a deserted video games arcade and ten-pin bowling area. In the middle of the gleaming floor is a large aquarium. He walks towards the raised tank over polished marble that muffles his footsteps. Around him a few people glide about in the twilight. A large yellow tropical fish stares at him with an unblinking eye whilst rubbing its flank against the thick glass.

From a Kentucky Fried Chicken outlet he buys three drumsticks and a packet of fries. He is alone in the dining area. While he eats he reads the multiplex's posters. The usual Hollywood pap: superheroes and monsters, good triumphing over evil, love conquering all. He considers whether to go and see a movie – time is something he certainly has. In the foyer of the multiplex scores of old people fuss around the refreshment counter. A grey-haired couple catches his eye. The husband – so he assumes – clutches his wife's hand; she laughs at something he says. Probably married fifty years and still holding hands, he thinks. He turns away, irritated. He decides not to: to sit alone in a cinema on a Monday morning surrounded by pensioners – for that he is not yet ready.

An escalator carries him up to the shopping levels. Here there are more people and the lights are brighter. The air smells expensive, like that in the restroom of an upmarket hotel. 'Silent Night' warbles through the public address system. The shopfronts are festooned with Christmas decorations and gift-wrapped boxes and, suspended high above from the ceiling, are four plastic reindeer and a large sleigh. He's never liked shopping centres and, coupled with this early Christmas cheer, it is almost too much to bear.

His precautions have been in vain. When he goes into Pick 'n Pay he sees Sonja, one of Louise's friends, approaching from the direction of the checkout. She hasn't seen him yet and he considers turning around, but then her glance falls and fixes on him. Two weeks earlier he had called her, but she couldn't or wouldn't tell him anything of Louise's whereabouts.

'Hello, Paul,' she says when she reaches him. She seems nervous and fidgets with an earring. 'Fancy seeing you here.'

He keeps it light. 'You know me, always one for new experiences.' He asks after her husband and children. While they talk an idea forms in his mind.

'Let's not stand here. How about a coffee?' he asks.

She glances at her watch. 'I don't know, I have to be somewhere at twelve.'

'Come on, one coffee, that's all.' He hates the pleading undertone he hears in his voice.

While they walk to the coffee shop, he remembers an incident at a party a year or so earlier. He had been alone in the kitchen when Sonja came in, cheeks flushed and eyes glowing. She stood on tiptoe and reached above his head to take a glass from a shelf; on her breath he smelled wine. She seemed to lose her footing and fell against him, her breasts pressing against his chest and her hip against his groin. He felt her strawberry-blonde hair against his cheek, her breath hot in his neck. For a few, long seconds they froze, undecided, neither advancing or retreating. He wondered for weeks afterwards what would have happened if they hadn't heard their host's voice approaching from the living room. Whenever they'd met since he had sensed a heightened alertness, maybe a guilty awareness, between them.

They go into the Seattle Coffee Shop. Large hessian sacks seemingly filled with coffee beans are stacked around the restaurant. A young waitress in dungarees approaches them over the wooden floor. She flashes sparkling teeth and a fake American 'Hi guys' at them, then escorts them to a table at the far end of the restaurant. This side of the restaurant overlooks the highway, but a thick ceiling-height window dampens the noise and glare of the traffic.

They order two cappuccinos. Sonja talks non-stop but avoids one topic. He waits for the opening he knows will come; he is ready when it does.

'Have you lost weight?' she asks.

He gives a small smile and holds her eyes. 'Well, as you know, things haven't exactly been going my way lately.'

She slides her hand over his and squeezes it. 'I'm sorry, Paul. I really am.'

To his embarrassment he feels his eyes moistening; he looks out of the window at the cars rushing by.

They sit silently for a minute or so. Then, without looking at him, she says, 'I heard that she's working in London. Don't ask me more, that's all I know, and you didn't hear it from me.'

MR VAN VUUREN: Let's continue. During your hospitalisation your commanding officer visited you. Would you read into the record the paragraph which relates to that meeting?

MR DU TOIT: 'Colonel Visser came to see me with Captain Harris, whom he introduced as being with Military Intelligence. Colonel Visser explained to me that existing police methods to combat the enemy forces operating inside South Africa were no longer effective. The Government had therefore decided to attack these elements in a more covert manner. Colonel Visser then said that there was another way in which I could take part in the war effort. This would be to assist Military Intelligence in its surveillance and destabilisation of the End Conscription Campaign - ECC - organisation.

'Captain Harris said that the ECC's campaign of encouraging school-leavers and students to ignore their conscription call-ups posed a serious threat to the defence capability of the country, as the largest part of the Defence Force's manpower consisted of conscripts. He also said that the ECC's efforts undermined the morale of the civilian population, and that it was working with United Democratic Front activists and underground ANC structures to create political unrest in the country. Military Intelligence had found out that the ECC had recruited a network of sympathetic National Servicemen in the Defence Force, and that the ECC was passing on sensitive military information to ANC structures. The ECC was particularly active at the University of Cape Town, where several of its key organisers were students.

'Captain Harris said that, should I be willing to assist MI, I would be expected to enrol at UCT. Colonel Visser and Captain Harris gave me a week to make up my mind. A few days later I told them that I would do it.'

MR VAN VUUREN: What motivated your decision?

MR DU TOIT: I had joined Special Forces to play an active role in the war. I still wanted to do this. Also, I still had another year left on my Permanent Force contract, and I didn't want to sit around a base in a support role.

MR VAN VUUREN: Why do you think you specifically were chosen for this role?

MR DU TOIT: I guess that because of my age MI felt that I could blend in as a student. And also because I had some experience of covert operations.

MR VAN VUUREN: In paragraph 8 you deal with your enrolment at UCT in February 1986 for a commerce degree. Can you tell us how you first made contact with the ECC?

MR DU TOIT: During my first few weeks at UCT I made a point of signing ECC petitions and saying in public that I would disobey any call-ups for future military service. As it happened, I met Mr André Pretorius, who was at high school with me, and who had gone directly to university after leaving school. He was now one of the campus organisers of the ECC. He introduced me to the other members of the organising committee of the ECC. I soon started distributing pamphlets and posters, speaking at meetings, setting up sound equipment for rallies and so on.

MR VAN VUUREN: Can I interrupt you there? Were Mr Pretorius and his colleagues not suspicious of your credentials, your objectives? After all, you had been a recce. Did they not question this change of heart?

MR DU TOIT: No, they were quite naïve. I quickly convinced them that I supported their cause. In any case, they didn't know that I had been in Special Forces, as we had been forbidden to tell civilians. I told them I had become disillusioned with the policies of the Government and the Defence Force. I also told them that I was bitter about my injury. There were also quite a few other ex-National Servicemen who were active members of the ECC. The ECC was only too glad to recruit more of us to their cause.

MR VAN VUUREN: Thank you. In paragraph 10 you go into more detail about the activities of Military Intelligence with regard to the ECC. Please read this into the record.

MR DU TOIT: 'My Project Officer was Captain Harris, who was attached to the Communications Operations division within MI. I met with Captain Harris on an ad hoc basis several times a month. My objectives were to infiltrate the ECC and to provide information on its activities, membership, meetings and sources of funding.'

MR VAN VUUREN: What did Military Intelligence do with this information?

MR DU TOIT: It helped MI to combat the ECC with counter-revolutionary propaganda and psychological warfare.

MR VAN VUUREN: Can you be more specific? What did propaganda and psychological warfare entail?

MR DU TOIT: There were many elements. Propaganda, for example, could involve MI secretly passing around pamphlets which said that the ECC had hidden links to Moscow, that it supported violence, or that certain of its leaders were homosexual, things like that. It could also be the planting of negative stories about the ECC with journalists at friendly newspapers and the SABC. Psychological warfare was things like damaging the cars of ECC organisers, that kind of thing.

MR VAN VUUREN: Thank you. We now come to the events that you are seeking amnesty for. Before we continue, how old were you when the incident in question occurred?

MR DU TOIT: I was 22.

MR VAN VUUREN: So you were still a very young man at that stage?

MR DU TOIT: Yes.

MR VAN VUUREN: Thank you. Could you now please read paragraph 11 into the record?

MR DU TOIT: 'The Government declared a national State of Emergency in June 1986. Shortly afterwards Captain Harris informed me that it had been decided at the highest level to disrupt the ECC once and for all so that it would stop operating. The countrywide campaign and harassment against ECC organisers was therefore going to be stepped up. The State of Emergency legislation also made it illegal for any person or organisation to make statements that undermined or discredited the system of compulsory military service. While the ECC itself was not banned, a number of ECC activists were detained or served with restriction orders, while others went into hiding. To strengthen my cover I was also seemingly detained for three weeks in September 1986. But actually during this period I stayed in the Special Forces base in Langebaan.'

MR VAN VUUREN: What happened after you returned to university?

MR DU TOIT: I soon found out that, despite the State of Emergency and the detentions, the ECC was remobilising and that meetings with ANC and UDF activists were still taking place. At these meetings plans were being made for mass action and protest rallies. Captain Harris and I discussed various ways of disrupting these meetings. We did not make any decision, however, as Captain Harris had to consult with the Military Intelligence command structure.

MR VAN VUUREN: Could you now please read paragraph 12 into the record.

MR DU TOIT: 'On 2 November 1986 I met Captain Harris at a restaurant in Bellville. At this meeting he informed me that a project against the ECC and UDF had been authorised. The project would involve detonating a limpet mine of Eastern Bloc origin at the Mitchells Plain community centre where a meeting was going to take place on Thursday, 27 November 1986. The limpet mine would be detonated by remote control after the meeting had ended, when the hall was empty, to prevent any casualties.'

MR VAN VUUREN: Did Captain Harris indicate who specifically within Military Intelligence authorised the project?

MR DU TOIT: No, he did not, and I did not ask.

MR VAN VUUREN: Why detonate a bomb to disrupt a meeting? Why not just send in the police to break it up under the State of Emergency regulations?

MR DU TOIT: It was felt a detonation would send the strongest possible signal to the ECC that it should stop its subversive activities. Obviously the hall would also be destroyed, which would prevent them from having meetings there again. And Military Intelligence would also be able to undermine the peaceful credentials of the ECC by planting stories that the limpet mine was part of a terrorist arms cache, and that it had accidentally detonated.

MR VAN VUUREN: Thank you. So it was your clear understanding that the detonation should not cause the death of anyone?

MR DU TOIT: Yes. The project was not aimed at specific individuals, but at disrupting the subversive activities of the ECC.

MR VAN VUUREN: To be more specific - there was no order that the project should result in the death of anyone?

MR DU TOIT: No, nothing like that. I would not have taken part in such a thing.

LONDON

6

He wakes up in a cold room with a high ceiling. The air smells damp. He is stiff and his mouth tastes ashy. Under him he feels the plastic mattress cover. Across the room is a washbasin and a mirror, on the side table next to the bed a telephone and a London guide book. He gets up and walks to the window. He touches the radiator under the window; it has cooled during the night. With his palm he rubs an opening on the misted-over window. Instead of a garden and a sunlit pool he sees a dustbin-filled courtyard four floors below and metal ducts running up a concrete wall towards a grey sky. He has travelled from summer to winter, sunshine to gloom.

He showers in the bath, shaves, then goes downstairs. He eats breakfast in the overheated dining room with a few other solitary diners. Everyone avoids eye contact. The room's thick windows shudder every now and then from the passing convoys of red buses and black cabs in the street.

He unfolds a map on the table. He will begin at the South African High Commission, he decides. In truth, he has no idea where else to start; a week ago in the coffee shop he had pressed Sonja for more information, but she hadn't budged. It takes him a few minutes to trace the route from his Russell Square hotel to Trafalgar Square – the location of South Africa House – in the maze of streets on the map, the names of which are printed so small that he has to peer down to decipher them.

Why she chose London of all places, he does not know. She has been to England only once, a year earlier, to attend an IT conference in a town somewhere near London. And as far as he is aware she does not know anyone in London.

Outside it is raining, a fine drizzle that is more damp than wet, and a cold breeze plucks at his anorak. He walks in the direction of Tottenham Court Road. He scans the grim faces of the passers-by, even though he knows that it's a futile exercise. The overcast city is intimidating. Everywhere are monumental granite and stone buildings, the legacy of the empire that had crushed the Boer republics a century before.

It is his second time in London. Three years before he and four other DAB traders accompanied some clients to a South Africa–England rugby international at Twickenham. But that weekend he had seen little of London: the hotel near Green Park, three or four smoky pubs, the rugby stadium lapped by a grey sea of terraced houses.

The pedestrian traffic in Tottenham Court Road is heavy, and he feels hemmed in by the press of people. He turns into a side street. Soon he is lost, despite his map. Some streets look promising, only to meander off into another direction or to peter out in little squares or circles. The street names are odd – Brewer's Yard, St Giles, New Compton – and give no clue as to where they lead. At a traffic circle he is confronted with streets running off in seven different directions. Nowhere is a landmark that he can use to take bearings from, and in the narrow streets bland concrete structures jostle for space with imposing, centuries-old buildings. And it is here, in this labyrinth, that he will have to find her, he thinks, suppressing a pang of doubt.

He eventually ends up at Covent Garden, the garden of which doesn't seem to justify its prominent place on the map, and here a bobby directs him to Trafalgar Square. A few minutes later damp pigeons flutter out of his way as he crosses the wet square.

Mounted over a side entrance of South Africa House is a gold-coloured springbok. Rain glistens on its metal flanks and face, giving it a disconsolate air, as if it is unhappy to find itself stranded in this unfamiliar terrain. And carved – surprisingly – in the wall of the large grey edifice is the old national motto 'Eendragt maakt magt' – In unity is strength.

He goes in through two large wooden doors and walks up a short marble staircase. At the top of the stairs hangs a large portrait of the prim-mouthed new President looking displeased about something. But, other than the drooping desk flags, the decor of the small lobby is that of the old South Africa: polished parquet floors, dark wood-panelling, potted rubber plants.

Behind a counter a braided receptionist is talking on the phone. He sits down on a chair in the waiting area. Fanned out on a side table are tourist brochures: *South Africa – a World in One Country*, *Discover the Rainbow Nation*, *The Garden Route Experience*. He glances at the photos of Mandela, Table Mountain, bare-breasted tribal women, white beaches, golf courses, lions. He picks up the *SA Times*, which, he reads, is a free newspaper for South African expatriates in the United Kingdom. An article catches his eye: a firm of immigration solicitors estimates that at least half a million ex-South Africans live in the Greater London area.

When the receptionist puts down the phone he walks over to the counter. She looks up at him and, before he has a chance to speak, frowns and says, 'If you've lost your passport, go down the road to our Consulate Section at Whitehall 15.' Her accent is not English, the flat vowels and inflections of her speech are those of the coloured Afrikaans-speakers of the Western Cape.

'Goeiemore. Nee, dis nie hoekom ek hier is nie,' he replies.

Her frown deepens; it seems his feeble attempt at establishing a rapport is not appreciated. 'I don't speak that language,' she says.

'I'm sorry.' He feigns a smile. 'I've just arrived in London and I'm looking for someone who came over here a few weeks ago. Does the embassy keep any sort of record of South Africans in London, some kind of database?'

She looks at him incredulously, shakes her head. 'I don't know who gave you that idea, but it is not our job to keep track of all you people who come here.'

He notes the *you people*, but holds his smile – he might need to come here again. 'Any idea how I would go about finding someone?'

Again she shakes her head, then looks over his shoulder. 'No idea. Now, if you don't mind, there are other people waiting.'

Outside it is darker than before. The leaden sky presses down on the wet city. Most of the pedestrians are dressed in some shade of black or grey, and the streets and buildings seem to be covered in a dull film of grime. He goes into a Starbucks. He drinks his coffee at a table facing the pavement and watches the never-ending stream of passers-by who drift past like schools of pale deep-sea fish.

It is not going to be easy, that much he now realises. The past week had been a busy one; between making travel arrangements, putting his furniture in storage and selling his car he hadn't given much thought to how he was going to find her. A formidable task – a city of eight million people, amongst which there are hundreds of thousands of South Africans, half a million even, if the *SA Times* is to be believed.

He'll have to infiltrate the South African expatriate community, he decides; eventually he is sure to meet someone who knows or has met her. But that could mean a stay of several months and he can't afford to stay in a hotel that long. He opens the *SA Times* he took from South Africa House and thumbs through to the accommodation section.

There is no answer at the first two numbers that he phones from his hotel room. At the third listing – *Single room (80 pw) in house (West Kensington) with 4 Saffas* – Steve answers. The room is still available, he can come around and see it that evening after seven, when the other guys will also be there.

Late afternoon he takes the tube to West Kensington. The carriage is crowded and the air smells sour, a grim aroma of sweat and breath. As instructed, he disembarks at Baron's Court tube station. From there he follows Steve's directions, which take him through Hammersmith Cemetery and a council estate, then into Whippet Road. He is a few minutes early, and walks past the unpainted terraced house at Number 303. Across the street is a small park with rusty-looking climbing frames and slides. The trampled-down grass of the park looks oily in the yellow glare of the streetlight, and on a leafless branch a plastic bag flutters in the wind. At the end of the street are small shops and a large block of flats with washing suspended across the balconies. He turns around and walks back to the house.

A tall, thin guy – early twenties, he estimates – with red hair and freckles opens the front door and introduces himself as Steve. He follows him down a corridor and into the kitchen. Around the table are three other youths about Steve's age. Steve does the introductions. He makes an effort to remember their names: Marius is shaven-headed, Chris looks like a prop forward, JB's cheeks and neck bear the scars of teenage acne.

They sit down at the kitchen table. 'So, Paul, how long are you over here for?' Steve asks.

He considers his answer carefully. 'Not sure, six months or so maybe. I want to work and save some money to travel through Europe.' Marius and Chris glance at each other. He senses what they're thinking: he is at least a decade older than they are, not the usual age for a backpacker. 'Just got divorced, needed some space,' he adds.

JB nods. 'Women,' he sighs. 'Can't live with them, can't live without them.'

He smiles. JB doesn't strike him as someone who has had many skirmishes on that front. The atmosphere lightens. Steve offers him a beer; they ask a few more questions, establish that he can pay a month in advance.

Steve shows him the house. The threadbare grey carpeting is stained and the walls need a fresh coat of paint. JB and Marius share a room on the second floor; Chris and Steve have their own rooms on the top floor, next to the room which is to let. He walks past the single bed and built-in cupboard and looks out of the window – a small, overgrown garden and the back of a row of red-brown terraced houses. Meagre but sufficient.

In the kitchen he hands Steve £320 and gets a front door key in return. He takes leave of his new housemates, then walks to the tube station. At the corner of street he turns around and looks back. Outside the park a group of teenagers in shiny tracksuits are passing cans of beer and cigarettes around, overhead the lights of half a dozen planes crawl slowly across the sulphurous sky. So you fall, he thinks, now he is truly part of the flotsam and jetsam of this city.

7

After checking out of the hotel the next morning he buys a sleeping bag and pillow from a department store in Oxford Street; by noon he has moved into the house. Later in the afternoon he goes out to buy food – according to Steve one of the house traditions is that a new lodger makes dinner for everyone on his first day. He puts two chickens in the oven, mixes a green salad, steams instant rice.

In the evening the others return from work. They talk little while they eat at the kitchen table. When the food is finished, Steve lights a cigarette and looks at him. 'So, any idea what you're going to do?'

'Not really, I'm in the market for anything.'

'Nothing going at my place, I'm afraid.' Steve is a barman somewhere in Central London.

Marius also shakes his head. A scratch golfer, he teaches at a driving range. JB, who like Chris is a construction worker, says, 'We can speak to our foreman. I'm sure he can use another hand, we're already behind schedule on this building. It's shit work, but there's lots of overtime money.'

Chris looks at him and asks, 'Did you do your National Service?'

'Yes.'

'Where?'

'Saldanha, in the Navy. Why?'

'Someone I know works for a security company in North London. He says they're always looking for guys who have some military or police experience. Easy job, and the pay's not too bad. I can give you his number if you want.'

'Why don't you guys go for it?' he asks.

JB laughs, exposing a large gap between his two front teeth. 'Wasn't in the army. Thanks to Mandela I dodged that one.'

He remembers – the new government ended conscription in 1994.

The windows of the kitchen have misted up. Steve pulls open a drawer and takes out a plastic pouch. 'Durban Poison, my hometown's best,' he smiles. He spreads the marijuana on a sheet of newspaper with a photo of a chubby, bare-breasted blonde.

'So, Paul, how're things back home?' Chris asks. Sturdy and stolid, with large, blunt fingers, Chris reminds him of the farm boys he had served with, uncomplaining soldiers who had adapted easily to the discomfort and routine of military life. 'Are the non-swimmers still fucking it up?'

'Okay. Other than crime, things aren't too bad.'

Chris says, 'My dad reckons I shouldn't come back. He says there's no future for us in South Africa.'

Marius shakes his head. 'Come on, Chris, that's unfair. Give the guys a chance. Things were in pretty bad shape when they took over.'

'Fuck off, what you talking about?' says Chris, his face reddening. 'We gave them a country that was working – banks, roads, power stations, telephones, hospitals, that kind of thing. South Africa would have been in the same mess as the rest of fucking Africa if we hadn't been in charge for the past three hundred and fifty years.'

JB rolls his eyes. 'Here we go again.'

He listens with little interest to Chris and Marius arguing. How many times has he listened to similar arguments around braaivleis fires and at bar counters? And those who argued the most vociferously were usually those who had been oblivious to what had underpinned their suburban lives in South Africa. These boys, for that's really what they are, had been in primary school while he was slogging through the sand and bush and dust of Angola, in that protracted struggle which his generation had been conscripted into, had believed in, had died in.

Steve lights the zol and inhales deeply. 'Don't worry, be happy,' he says, slowly exhaling a cloud of smoke. JB takes the zol from Steve, drags on it, then hands it on. He passes it on to Marius without smoking. Steve raises an eyebrow. 'No worries, the more for us.'

Later he goes up to his room. In bed he lies listening to his housemates moving about the house. Once again he is on a mission of sorts, he thinks, but what are the chances of picking up the spoor of his quarry in this unfamiliar landscape?

At four in the morning he wakes with a start; he dreamt of something or someone chasing him, of fire and soot and fear. He feels a draught on his face and gets up and goes to the bedroom window. Cold air is seeping in through a gap between the frame and glass. He wets a wad of toilet paper in the bathroom and plasters the gap. In the distance he hears a police siren. He stands at the window and listens. The siren gets closer, then suddenly stops somewhere nearby. He waits a while and, hearing nothing else, goes back to bed.

He can't fall asleep again. He thinks of his new housemates. Earlier in the evening the dagga and their argument had stirred a memory, but the recollection had been fleeting. Now he remembers: a winter afternoon after rugby practice, he and André driving out of the schoolyard on their motorcycles, his tog bag balanced on the petrol tank between his grazed knees.

André waved him down at the first street corner. 'Want to try some dagga?'

He pushed up his visor. 'Where?'

André led the way to a block of flats in a neighbouring suburb. They kept their helmets on and went up the fire escape stairs to the flat concrete roof of the building. Two black men, dressed in green flat-boy uniforms, were sitting on metal chairs outside their room in the middle of the roof.

'Dumela,' André greeted them.

The men nodded cautiously and remained seated.

'Do you know where we can get the dagga?' André asked.

Both men shook their heads. 'Aikôna, kleinbasie – we don't know about things like that,' said one.

André took a crumpled ten rand note from his pocket and waved it in the air. 'Are you sure?'

The two men spoke to each other in rapid Sotho, and André winked at him. They had come to a decision, it seemed, as one of them stood up and walked to the fire escape. He glanced down, then walked to the front of the roof and looked over the edge. He turned around and nodded before entering the small room.

Inside it smelled of Lifebuoy soap and pipe tobacco. There were two neatly made up beds that were raised on bricks, probably to prevent the tokoloshe from clambering up while they were sleeping. One of the men prised loose a floor tile, took a Lion matchbox from the recess and handed it to André.

They rode to the top of the koppie overlooking their suburb. Far below, swimming pools sparkled in the afternoon sun, and here and there he could see a postage stamp-sized tennis court in a lush garden. On the horizon a pall of smoke shrouded the black townships.

André extracted the tobacco from two cigarettes, pushed in the dagga with a match and twisted the ends of the cigarettes so the dagga wouldn't fall out.

The dagga pips crackled as they inhaled furiously. The smoke chafed their lungs, but the expected high did not come. 'My brother says that it sometimes doesn't work the first time,' André said after they had each finished a second zol.

He lifted the matchbox to his nose. 'I wonder. This doesn't smell like dagga to me. It smells like grass – I mean, like garden grass.'

André took the matchbox, sniffed, then laughed. 'Those fuckers, they saw us coming.'

'Ja, you can never trust a fucking houtkop,' he said. 'Look what happened to Piet Retief and his men. Dingaan persuaded them to leave their guns outside his kraal when they came to negotiate with him about land – then his impis battered them to death.'

'That's one way of looking at it,' André said.

'What other way is there?' he said irritably. He suspected that André would once again present him with a different version of history than the one they were taught at school. Once he had overheard his father saying to dinner guests that André's father, a university professor, was one of those left-leaning wayward Afrikaners who always questioned and criticised everything the government did.

'Well, look at it from Dingaan's point of view. He thought they were coming to steal the land.' André lay back and rested his head against a boulder. 'And wasn't he right?'

'Bullshit. They came to buy land, not to steal it.'

'Buy? Some guns and tobacco for as much land as you could see? The blacks didn't believe that anyone could own land. It belonged to everyone, and their chief was the guardian.'

'Too bad. A deal is a deal. And anyway, in Africa it's the rule of the strongest.'

André lit another cigarette. 'You're starting to sound like your father.'

'That's because he's right.'

'Your problem is that you see everything in black and white, but life's not like that. Don't believe everything you read in *Die Oggendblad* or see on SABC. Read some books, a couple of English newspapers – maybe then your eyes will open a bit.'

'Reading books! What, like you, my nose always stuck in a book?' He shook his head. 'No thanks. Books are for people who are afraid of life. You must live life, not read about it.'

André stood up. 'Whatever you say.' He looked at the darkening sky. 'I'd better get home.'

They had parted on a strained note, each going in a different direction.

Even now, eighteen years later, André's remark rankles. Maybe back then he hadn't been aware of the mounting tension in the country. But hadn't South Africa always been, and wouldn't it always be, about black and white? Apartheid had been abolished a decade earlier, skin colour not. The old laws had new cloaks: affirmative action, black economic empowerment, racial employment and sports quotas – the building blocks of the new promised land. The rainbow nation, but did a rainbow have white in it?

And André, whose face he can no longer clearly see, what would he say to André should they meet in an afterlife, if there was such a thing? But what use were words? Words were for politicians, those peddlers of dreams, dreams of patriotism and love of the volk or the Rainbow Nation, dreams that were ultimately just that.

8

Two days later Steve throws a party; he is turning twenty-two. Several dozen guests, mostly South Africans, but also some Australians and New Zealanders, arrive well provisioned with beer, wine and alcopops. He is the oldest at the party, but he makes an effort to mingle with his countrymen. Not to be social, but in an attempt to find out whether they know anything about Louise.

Later he stands at the entrance of the lounge and watches the heaving crowd dancing to music he doesn't know. He feels a tap on his shoulder, turns around.

'What's your name?' a girl a head shorter than him and with full lips shouts over the music, a can of beer in her hand.

'Paul.'

She shakes his hand. 'Karen.' Then she pulls him into the lounge. 'Come dance.'

He bobs and weaves as best he can but feels awkward and out of step. Karen dances with abandon, twirling around and lifting her arms in the air, only slowing down occasionally to sip from her can. He takes her measure: blonde-brown hair, a wide mouth, ample breasts; if she shed a couple of pounds and applied some make-up she would probably be quite pretty. When the song ends he starts to move away, but she pulls him back. The next song is a slower one, and around them couples move closer to each other. Karen puts her arms around his neck, her breasts pressing against his stomach. And now a memory of another party comes to him, so vivid that for a moment he imagines it is Louise who is in his arms.

Before that party he and two friends had downed six beers and a flask of wine in a nearby park. This time André was not with them; according to him, his motorcycle was in for servicing and his father was going to bring him to the party.

The party was in full swing when they got there and couples were dancing in the garage. He walked into the courtyard that bordered the garage. André stood with his back towards him – to startle him he slapped the back of André's legs with his helmet. Only then did he see whom André was talking to – the new girl from Cape Town. She was wearing stovepipe jeans and a jumper with a rhinestone pattern.

'Louise, I don't know if you've met this idiot?' André said.

She examined him, the corners of her mouth turned up in a slight smile, and shook her head.

'Well, this is Paul, not really someone that you want to know.'

She put her hand out towards him. 'Now why is that?' she asked, her eyes not wavering from his. While he was still scrambling for a retort, 'Radar Love' started up and André quickly led her to the garage.

And so one's life shifts course, he thinks. A look, a few words, and something germinates. But all he was aware of then was a shortness of breath, and a fervent desire to talk to her again.

From outside the garage he watched her and André dancing, and awaited his chance. Ten minutes later, while André was talking to someone else, he pounced. 'Would you like to dance?' he asked, his voice suddenly hoarse.

She smiled. 'Okay.' She tapped André on the back. 'I'm going to dance with your friend.'

André nodded. 'Sure, sure,' he said. But he seemed annoyed.

Suddenly realising something, he asked, 'Did you come with André?' as they walked away.

'Yes, his father brought us.'

So that was the reason André hadn't been with them earlier. And that evening the rivalry between André and him started, a rivalry never acknowledged, but a rivalry just the same.

In the garage Louise made no attempt at conversation, seemingly content to wait in silence for the music to begin. Thankfully, someone put on a record and dimmed the lights. But it was 'Hey Jude', a slow song, which meant they would have to hold each other while they danced. He looked at her: a girl who was not going out with you could always change her mind if it was a close dance. But she moved towards him. He put his arms around her, one hand on her lower back, the other on her shoulder blade. Under his left hand he felt the strap of her bra. She was soft and warm in his arms and her hair smelt of apples. They swayed to the slow beat of the song. Around them couples who were going steady started kissing. He closed his eyes and pulled her closer.

Her pelvis brushed against his groin; embarrassed, he tried to turn his hip towards her. But she moved with him, holding him tighter, making full contact with him. It was impossible for her not to notice, he realised.

When the music died down and he opened his eyes, André stood next to them. 'Song's over. My turn, china.'

Reluctantly he let go. Louise stepped away, her face flushed. 'Thanks, Paul.'

Later that evening, back at home, he held his shirt against his face. Mingled with the smell of deodorant and sweat and smoke there was another scent, a fresh, clean scent.

But Karen smells of cigarette smoke. When the song ends she takes him by the hand and leads him out of the lounge. 'Show me your room,' she commands. So she knows that he lives here; she must have asked one of his housemates. He can guess what's coming, but he doesn't care. Tonight he doesn't want to be alone. She is better than nothing, and he has had his fill of nothing.

Steve winks when they pass him on the stairs. In his room Karen slips her hand in the pocket of her jeans and extracts a small pink pill. 'Happy medicine,' she says, and bites the pill in half. She holds out her hand to him. 'Want some?'

He shakes his head.

She shrugs her shoulders and swallows both halves with a swig of beer. She takes something else from her pocket, then perches on the edge of his bed. He stands at the window and watches as she removes the dagga pips and then rolls a zol. No older than nineteen, twenty maybe, but an old hand, he thinks.

She lights up and pulls deep and long. 'Want some?' she says, keeping the smoke in.

He doesn't like drugs, not being in control, but tonight that's exactly what he wants. The smoke burns his lungs, but again he inhales deeply, keeping the smoke inside for as long as possible.

She laughs. 'Slowly, slowly, that's strong stuff. Leave some for me.' She pats the space next to her on the bed. 'Come sit here. I won't bite.'

He sits down next to her. On her forehead is a small pimple. The dagga takes effect, the music from downstairs sounding better, his thoughts slowing down, his face numbing. Then Karen's lips are on his. She pushes him onto his back and slips her tongue into his mouth. She tastes of dagga and chewing gum.

After a while she pulls away. 'This is the best time to do it, don't you think?'

'I wouldn't know.'

She laughs, a girlish whinny, and pulls off her shirt, exposing firm breasts with large brown areolae and a ring of puppy fat around her midriff. She stands up and peels off her jeans. He glimpses a strip of black pubic hair: a bottle blonde. He sits up, reaches forward; she shudders when he touches her. She unbuckles his belt and kneels between his legs. He feels her teeth nibbling expertly on him. Her head moves industriously and he feigns enthusiasm, but after a while she lifts her head and looks up. 'What's wrong?'

He feels sorry for her, and embarrassed. 'The dagga – sometimes happens.'

'Just my luck,' she says and lies down next to him. 'You're not gay, are you?' She runs her hand through his hair. 'Seems most of the nice guys are these days.'

He tries to lift his head to answer, but it feels heavy, and the room moves under him. He closes his eyes to shut out the nausea. Against him Karen's warm skin feels good; he pulls her closer. The bass of the music downstairs makes the bed vibrate.

When he wakes she is gone. His mouth is dry. The music has stopped and the house is quiet. It is three-thirty in the morning. He is hungry, and his bladder is full. He fastens his trousers and goes downstairs to the kitchen. Everywhere are empty bottles and cans and ground-out cigarette butts.

He walks out into the overgrown backyard. The sky glows yellow. Overhead a few scattered stars flicker weakly; he doesn't recognise any. A gust of wind rolls a beer can against the kitchen steps. He pulls up his zip and goes back into the kitchen, where he drinks deep from the tap. Afterwards he eats four slices of buttered toast.

He goes back to his room and crawls into his sleeping bag. On his pillow is a long blonde hair, on his fingers the smell of the girl. He feels deflated, out of kilter, the aftermath of something illicit. But it is not the first time. During seven years of marriage there were two others: a secretary in his car after an office function, a year or two later a stripper at a stag party, drunken fumblings that had made no lasting impression. The tightness in his chest is back, and the familiar memories are surfacing. He tries to resist; he knows he will not sleep again if he succumbs. But he fails. He stares into the darkness, and the longing squeezes his chest like a vice.

MR VAN VUUREN: Let us now continue with the incident in question. Will you please read paragraph 13 into the record?

MR DU TOIT: 'The plan was to plant two limpet mines of Soviet origin in the hall. One would be detonated by remote control, but the other one would be left for the police to discover. The project team would consist of me, Captain Harris and a civilian surrogate. I was to be the liaison with the surrogate, who would plant the limpet mines and then detonate one of them. Captain Harris told me that a coloured criminal called Tommy had been chosen as the surrogate. Tommy was under the impression that he would be working for a right-wing organisation. We discussed various other aspects of the project. Captain Harris had obtained the keys to a side door of the hall, which he then handed to me, together with R20,000.'

MR VAN VUUREN: Did Captain Harris tell you why a civilian surrogate had to be used?

MR DU TOIT: He said it was to ensure a proper cut-off between the Defence Force and the project. Also, as the hall was in Mitchells Plain, a Coloured area, it would obviously be easier for Tommy to move around the area without attracting attention.

MR VAN VUUREN: But what about you? Why use you? Wouldn't you provide a link to Military Intelligence and the Defence Force?

MR DU TOIT: For all intents and purposes I was a student. And I would use a cover identity when I met with the surrogate. The risk was considered acceptable.

MR VAN VUUREN: Thank you. In paragraph 14 you outline your meeting with Tommy, and the events thereafter. Please read this into the record.

MR DU TOIT: 'I met Tommy in a room at the Newlands Hotel on 14 November 1986. I introduced myself as Pieter Brand. I told Tommy that my organisation thought that the Government was too soft on the UDF, and wanted to launch its own attacks on the UDF.'

MR VAN VUUREN: Let me interrupt there. What was your opinion of Tommy? Were you not concerned that a criminal was being used in such a sensitive project?

MR DU TOIT: I was not impressed with Tommy. He did not strike me as a reliable individual. But I accepted that it was a covert project and that sometimes we had to make use of people like that. In any case, his tasks were relatively simple.

MR VAN VUUREN: But why would Tommy co-operate? After all, he was member of the Coloured community. Why would he want to help a White right-wing organisation?

MR DU TOIT: Money. For money. Tommy was going to be paid R20,000 for his role in the project.

MR VAN VUUREN: Thank you. Please continue.

MR DU TOIT: 'I briefed Tommy on the project, and instructed him to make himself familiar with the terrain and the inside of the hall in the next few days. It was his responsibility to identify a hiding place for the limpet mines.

   'I also handed him the key that Captain Harris had given me, and R5,000. We arranged to meet again on Wednesday, 26 November.'

MR VAN VUUREN: Thank you. You then deal with the events of that day. Please read paragraph 15 into the record.

MR DU TOIT: 'On the morning of 26 November I drove to 4 Reconnaissance Regiment at Langebaan, where I collected two limpet mines and a remote detonator. At 19h00 that evening I met Tommy in the parking area of Muizenberg beach, as we had arranged, as it was close to the community hall. He confirmed that he had made himself familiar with the inside of the hall and its immediate surroundings. I handed him the limpet mines and instructed him in the correct use of the remote-control mechanism. I furthermore instructed him to detonate the limpet mine only when he was sure that the meeting was over, and that everyone had left the hall. From what I had previously established these meetings usually ended before 22h00, therefore a safe time to enter to detonate the limpet mine would probably be around 23h00. We arranged to meet again on Friday, 28 November at 10h00 at the same place, when I would hand over the rest of his payment.'

MR VAN VUUREN: Were you satisfied that Tommy clearly understood his instructions, that he clearly understood how to operate the remote control, and that he clearly understood that under no circumstances was he to detonate the limpet mine while there were still people in the hall?

MR DU TOIT: I was. We went through the plan a few times, and we did several trial runs with arming and operating the mechanism. The mechanism was relatively simple.

MR VAN VUUREN: Thank you. You then state that you returned to your residence in Cape Town. But you had no way of being sure that Tommy had in fact followed your instructions and planted the device. Weren't you concerned about this?

MR DU TOIT: No. Tommy knew that he wouldn't get the remaining R15,000 if he didn't follow my instructions.

MR VAN VUUREN: Thank you. Let me then ask you again — was it your impression that Tommy had clearly understood your instructions, and that the objective was not to injure or cause the death of people in the hall?

MR DU TOIT: That is correct. As I recall I spent nearly two hours with Tommy at our last meeting.

9

He phones Chris's security company contact and a meeting is arranged for him with Fergal Kennedy, the owner of Regal Protection Services. It is a fifteen-minute walk from Wembley tube station through a neigbourhood of dilapidated houses and cars to Regal's premises: three prefabricated buildings behind a chain-link fence. There are four white panel vans emblazoned with crowns parked in front of the buildings. Somewhere around the back of the buildings he hears dogs barking.

Fergal Kennedy is a sturdy middle-aged Irishman with close-cropped grey hair and a firm handshake. On the walls behind his tidy desk are framed photographs of Fergal in an army uniform; in one he sees a major's insignia on the shoulders.

Fergal notices him examining the pictures. 'Royal Irish, twenty years,' he says in a thick brogue, not unlike the burr of the Namaqualand Afrikaners. Fergal stretches back in his chair. 'So tell me about your background.' His *your* comes out as *jirr*.

When he is finished Fergal says, 'Well, you are certainly qualified.' He straightens a stack of papers in front of him. 'Look, I've always got work for the right man. There's nothing permanent right now, but one of my guards at the British Museum is going on leave on Thursday. What's your availability?'

'I can start immediately, Mr Kennedy.'

Fergal looks at him knowingly. 'But you're on a South African passport?'

He nods and remembers the stony-faced immigration officer at Heathrow and the stamp in his passport: *Leave to enter for six months – Employment and recourse to public funds prohibited.*

'How long are you going to be in London?'

'I'm not sure, six months maybe.'

'Then we'll put you on the books as a casual worker. Six pounds an hour in cash, no benefits but no tax either. You'll be issued with two uniforms. Keep them clean and in good shape.'

The fog lies thick in Whippet Road as he shuts the front door behind him on Thursday morning. He walks through Hammersmith Cemetery, his new boots creaking on the tarmac path as he passes the mossy gravestones.

Even at this early hour the carriage of the tube is crowded, mostly with glum office workers engrossed in their newspapers and books. Here and there a suited businessman is reading the *Financial Times*. Once he was a businessman of sorts, he thinks, but already that seems in the distant past. The other commuters look through him; in his uniform he has become invisible, just one more of the thousands of menial workers who service this city. Whenever the train stops at a station and the doors slide open he examines hopefully the faces of those getting on.

Massive pillars dwarf him as he walks up the steps of the British Museum. He tries to recall when last he visited a museum, but all he remembers is a primary school trip to the Voortrekker Museum in Pretoria.

A guard stops him – the museum is not yet open. He explains and is escorted by a second guard to a basement office. The head of security, a harassed-looking man who from time to time slips his hand into his trousers to rearrange his genitals, explains his duties. He is to be assigned to one of the Egyptian rooms, and his tasks are straightforward: ensure that the entrances remain unobstructed and that visitors don't climb on or damage the exhibits.

During the first hour there is only a trickle of visitors into the large hall with its massive statues and sculptures. Mid-morning the traffic increases; tourists photograph each other in front of the exhibits, tour groups trail guides, teachers shepherd flocks of noisy schoolchildren.

At midday he hears Afrikaans voices somewhere behind him. He turns around cautiously. It is nobody he knows, only a middle-aged couple standing next to the Rosetta Stone, the woman dressed in a blue parka and sensible slacks, her fleshy-faced male companion outfitted in a stonewashed leather jacket and denims.

He wonders what he would do if he meets an acquaintance from his previous life, say a client of DAB Securities, or a friend of his parents. What would he say, he thinks, imagining the awkward conversation that is sure to take place, the news eagerly spread back home. But such an encounter is unlikely – it is December and, back home, those people are probably already at the coast for the summer holidays.

He soon settles into a routine. From nine in the morning until eight in the evening he works at the museum; afterwards he visits pubs frequented by South Africans or attends South African parties he gets to hear about.

He criss-crosses London by tube, travelling to suburbs north and south of the Thames: Walthamstow, Leytonstone, Wood Green, Southfields, Putney, Roehampton, names that evoke rurality but always turn out to be built-up areas with endless rows of terraced houses and identical high streets.

The parties are in overcrowded flats and houses, houseshares similar to his own; the pubs have names like Barracuda, Springbok and Zulus. But no one knows or has heard of her. When he returns home, late at night, his housemates are usually asleep. On the days he doesn't work he washes and irons his clothes.

And everywhere he listens to the same conversations: laments about the miserable weather, the cost of living in London, the longing for home, doubts about the future of South Africa. His younger countrymen seem disorientated, alienated from the country where the certitudes of their elders have been trampled underfoot by the march of history, where the past is no guide to the future.

Late one evening, tired and half-drunk, he is in a pub near Covent Garden, watching and listening. And suddenly he is angry, angry that this is what it has come to, that this generation, the end product of the long struggle for an own language and country, have become merely the latest wave of colonised to break on the shores of this island. He is surprised by an unexpected concern for them. They are like newly hatched chicks, innocents abroad. What will become of them?

He thinks of the colossal statues he guards in the Egyptian Hall. A civilisation that flowered five thousand years ago and had endured for three thousand years. Weighed on that time scale, he thinks, the rise and fall of his people amounted to no more than a few grains of sand. And even of the Egyptian empire, which had lasted for thirty centuries, all that remained were museum exhibits and crumbling pyramids.

After a few weeks he realises that he is looking in the wrong places. Although he occasionally encounters someone his own age, the revellers are for the most part the generation after his. He is unlikely to find Louise amongst them.

He widens his search. A Google trawl yields scores of Louise du Toits and Louise Smits, but none in the United Kingdom. He now resorts to phoning London-based computer and financial services companies, but there are thousands of listings, and he manages to call only a dozen or so each day during his lunch break.

Three days before Christmas the guard whom he has been substituting for returns from leave. Regal now transfers him to North London to guard a street in Highgate for six nights a week.

His first shift is on Christmas Eve. He signs for a company patrol vehicle and follows a duty supervisor from Regal's offices to Highgate. In the back of the van is Rex, a lively young Alsatian that has been assigned to him. In Highgate the supervisor quickly shows him the ropes, then departs.

At eight he does his first foot patrol. It is cold, and he and the dog exhale bursts of vapour as they walk past the large detached houses with expensive cars in their gravelled driveways. Many of the houses are dark, but from some he hears the faint murmur of voices and the tinkle of music. When he returns he reads the tabloid newspaper the previous guard left behind. He reads the articles slowly; he is on duty for another eight hours. It is the usual news: football results, asylum seekers, tube strikes, house price rises.

He is reading an article on the risks of breast enlargement when a knock against the window startles him. An old woman bearing a tray is standing next to the van. He opens the door and gets out. She says something but the dog's barking drowns out her voice.

He bangs the roof of the van with his the palm of his hand. 'Rex, quiet!' He turns back to the woman. 'Sorry.'

She smiles. 'Merry Christmas. I'm Moira Wilson from Number 42.' She holds out the tray. 'It must be a long night for you. I thought you'd perhaps like some coffee.'

Thanks,' he says, surprised by the unexpected kindness.

'You're new, aren't you,' says Mrs Wilson, while he adds milk and sugar.

'Yes – first night.'

'And you're South African?'

He nods. It hadn't taken her long.

'My late husband and I visited Cape Town a couple of years ago. A lovely city.'

'Yes, it is.' He swallows the coffee and puts the mug back on the tray. 'Thank you.'

She looks down the road. 'Well, I'd better be getting back.'

He watches her shuffling away, then gets back into the van. Cape Town, he thinks. Nearly a year ago to the day.

For their summer holiday they had rented an apartment in Camps Bay for three weeks. One morning they drove out to Hermanus to spend the day with old university friends of Louise. They journeyed in silence – earlier they had argued, he not wanting to go, she insistent. The invitation had been extended and accepted months earlier; she had told him about it, she alleged.

A dozen or so cars were already parked in the driveway and street in front of the beach house. The front door was open and they walked towards the music. The other guests were clustered in small groups on the lawn, the meat was sizzling on the fire. In the distance the sea baked under a blue-white sky. Their host and Louise introduced him to people whose names he immediately forgot. Someone called her and she walked over to another group, leaving him at the fire with their host. He didn't know anyone at the party, which seemed to him a typical gathering of Cape Town pseudos, posers who affected an air of superiority.

He helped the host with the braai and later took the grilled meat through to the kitchen. While walking back he heard Louise's voice. She was on a couch in the lounge with her back towards him, talking to two other women, puffing on a cigarette. He felt his face, already hot from standing at the fire in the midday sun, glow even hotter. Without thinking he stepped into the room, plucked the cigarette from her fingers, and stubbed it out in an ashtray.

Louise turned around, her face flushing. 'What are you doing?' The other women stared at him.

'What are *you* doing? What did Dr Rubin say about smoking?' He wheeled around and strode out.

They were the first guests to leave after a strained lunch during which he and Louise did not talk to each other. It was only as they ascended Sir Lowry's Pass that she spoke, still looking out of her window at the coastal plain below. 'If you ever humiliate me like that again we're through.'

He shifted down a gear before answering. 'I'm sorry. I just don't want things to go wrong again.'

She turned towards him. 'Nothing's going to go wrong.'

Two months later she miscarried again.

He hasn't thought of that day for many months: Louise waking up in pain, the high-speed drive to Sandton Clinic in the early hours of Sunday, the long wait for the gynaecologist who had to be rousted from his suburban bed. But then he had always been good at forgetting, he thinks. And afterwards, in the days and weeks that followed, he didn't know what to say to her. How to talk of the dull ache of loss, the ever-present disappointment? Better just to press on, to forget.

He never talked about things that were important to him, Louise had once accused him. But he knows the instinct for concealment, the skill at not revealing himself, had been there from early on.

Suddenly, galvanised by an impulse he is unable to resist, he starts the van, then drives to a nearby service station. Inside the convenience store he inserts his call card into a payphone. His mother answers on the second ring, her voice as clear as if she's on a local call.

'Hello, Ma. Merry Christmas.'

A couple of seconds pass before she replies. 'Paul. I knew you would phone tonight. Are you all right? Why haven't you phoned? It's been more than a month.'

He can hear that she's on the verge of crying. 'I'm all right, Ma. Didn't you get my postcards?'

'I got one, nothing else.' She sounds tired. 'Why don't you phone?'

'Ma, I'm running out of money. I'm still in London, enjoying myself.' She believes he's on holiday.

'When are you coming back?'

'Ma, I must go, the line's very bad, and my money's run out. I just phoned to say merry Christmas.'

'Don't you want to speak to your father?'

'Bye, Ma,' he says, and replaces the receiver.

10

It is his second week at the new posting. A few minutes before midnight he cruises slowly down the street. As usual he sees nothing out of the ordinary, and most of the houses are dark. At the end of the road he turns around and drives back. But this time, halfway down the street, the van's lights fall on three people walking on the sidewalk. This is unusual – at night there is never much foot traffic, and at this late hour residents usually return home by car or cab.

As he gets closer he sees two men and a woman, who look as if they are arguing. Maybe drunks who have missed the tube. But then the woman runs into the road and waves him down. A stocky shaven-headed man wearing a black leather coat trots after her. Reluctantly he stops; he has no desire to get embroiled in a drunken squabble. By now the man has reached her and is pulling her back to the sidewalk. He gets out of the van and shines his torch on them. The woman is slender and about five-foot-six. She looks frightened.

'Please mister, help me,' she pleads in a foreign accent.

'What's the problem?' he asks.

The man lets go of her arm. 'Fuck off, mate, or do you want that torch up your arse?'

He ignores him and steps closer. 'What's wrong?' Her face is pale in the light of the street lamp; a girl really, nineteen, maybe twenty years old.

'I am au pair at Number 52,' she says, pointing to somewhere behind him. 'I don't know want they want, they follow me from station.'

The second man steps nearer. He is taller and bigger than the other man, and wears, despite the cold, a tight T-shirt that displays to good effect the bulging upper-arm muscles and neck of a regular iron-pumper. 'You heard what the man said, cunt. So be a good lad and fuck off.' A waft of alcohol hits his nostrils.

He grips the heavy metal torch tightly and with his other hand beckons the girl closer. 'Get in the van. I'll take you home.'

As she steps past him, he sees the shaven-headed man slip his right hand in the pocket of his coat, swaying on his feet as he does so. 'Oi, you fucking deaf, mate?' he says. The knife flashes in the street light when he pulls his hand out. 'Maybe you'll hear better when I cut your fucking bollocks off.'

Out of the corner of his eye he sees the second man put down his beer can on the tarmac. His heart is hammering in his chest. The first man is two paces away. He steps back until he feels the bonnet of the van pressing against his lower back. Two against one, and a knife. But they are drunk, he is not. The one with the knife looks faster, so he will have to be the first.

'You guys sure you want to do this?' he says, slapping the palm of his left hand with the torch, a familiar exhilaration coursing through him.

The two men look at each other, and the man with the knife shakes his head and grins. 'Fucking nutter!'

The body-builder chuckles and takes a step closer. He turns the torch towards him. Then the shaven-headed man lunges forward. He steps aside and brings the torch down hard on his elbow. The man grunts from the blow to his ulnar nerve and drops his knife. He swivels to his side. As he suspected, the body-builder's overdeveloped musculature slows him down. He waits for him, then feels the impact up to his shoulder and jaw as he slams the torch against his forehead. The man grunts and drops to his knees. He turns back to the shaven-headed man, who is trying to pick up the knife with his left hand. He drops the torch, grips the back of his coat with both hands, pulls it over his head, so that his coat is turned inside out, his head and arms trapped. He jerks the bundled figure towards him and lifts his knee; cartilage and teeth shatter. When he lets go of him the man falls sideways over a black bollard.

The body-builder is still on his knees, blood trickling down his face and dripping onto his T-shirt. He picks up his torch, walks closer, raises his arm. The man looks up with glassy eyes and lifts his hands. Now he hears the excited barking of the dog, and sees lights going on in houses on both sides of the street. He puts his palm against the man's forehead and pushes him on to his back. The girl suddenly darts away and runs down the street. From a house across the road a male voice shouts that the police are on their way.

He goes to the back of the van and lets out the dog. He sits and waits on a low garden wall, the dog's leash in his left hand. He wipes his hand on the wall; the torch he'll have to clean later. The shaven-headed man lies still, breathing noisily through his crushed nose; the body-builder is sitting upright, holding his head.

A pity about this, he thinks. He has attracted attention to himself, and now there will be an investigation, a court appearance probably, questions about his work permit, or lack thereof.

Only when a wailing police car turns into the street, a few minutes later, do a few residents come out of their properties, and he sees the girl and a middle-aged man walk towards him.

Two policemen get out of their vehicle. The older policeman examines the shaven-headed man, who has opened his eyes. The younger policeman radios in for an ambulance, then examines the flick knife. They question him first, the girl next. She is Monica, twenty-seven years old, older than she looks, and from the Czech Republic; she has been working in London as an au pair for the past three months. She has pronounced cheekbones and a thin nose, and her ears are the size of a child's. Monica confirms his version of events.

An ambulance arrives and the younger policeman gets into the back with the two injured men. When the ambulance and police vehicle drive away the residents drift back to their houses, except for a middle-aged man who comes over and shakes his hand.

'Alex Sturgeon. Monica works for us. I dread to think what could have happened if you hadn't intervened.' His accent is rich, the vowels rounded out.

Monica walks up to him. The streetlight reflects from her glossy black hair. She holds out her hand. 'Thank you.'

Her hand is soft and warm in his, and under his forefinger he feels a vein pulsing. She stands on tiptoe and kisses him on the cheek.

When she and the man turn into Number 52, she looks round and waves at him. The street is quiet again, the beer can on the tarmac the only evidence of what happened. He closes his eyes; he feels the onset of a headache.

He sleeps the next morning and most of the afternoon. When he wakes his headache has subsided, but he still feels tired. The house is quiet. Chris, JB and Marius are in South Africa for Christmas and New Year; it is only Steve and himself in the house. In any case, even when they are all there he sees little of his housemates, especially now that he works at night.

He fries an egg and sausages, makes coffee, irons his uniform: his daily routine. This is his life now, he thinks; a small life. He considers phoning a few more IT companies, but it is already half past four and he has to leave for work. Another wasted day.

When he reports for duty the supervisor informs him that Fergal

Kennedy wants to see him. He knocks on the open door and Fergal beckons him. When he sits down Fergal says, 'So what's this I hear? I got a call from a Mr Sturgeon.'

At the end of his account Fergal nods several times. 'Well done, well done. But in a situation like that I would have used the dog to pacify them. But then again, I wasn't there.' Fergal rises from his chair and shakes his hand. 'Keep up the good work.'

His talk with Fergal has delayed him and it is half-past six when he gets to Highgate. He parks halfway down the street, near the entrance to the golf club, and takes the dog on a foot patrol. Rex has been poorly trained. He strains and tugs at the leash and has to be kept away from the occasional pedestrians, grey-faced men and women with briefcases and bags who come from the direction of the tube station. He walks past the Sturgeon house but doesn't see Monica.

Later the lights in the houses go out, first at ground level, then on the upper floors, and the traffic decreases to a couple of cars every hour or so. Now comes the long part of the night, when nothing happens, and all there is to do is to think and remember. He is not unaccustomed to waiting, he thinks. But that was long ago and far away. He and two other operators had concealed themselves in a copse outside the enemy camp for five days, eighty yards from the nearest sentry post, eating, urinating, defecating and sleeping in the same place, noting the enemy battle order and routines, mopane flies tormenting them during the day and mosquitoes at night.

He fiddles with the tuner of the car radio, scanning the late-night talk shows and music channels. Suddenly he recognises a snatch of classical music and tunes into the station. It is a piece by an Italian composer whose name he can't remember, music his grandmother used to play, a piece that started with one or two organ notes, then joined by a harp, later by a score of violins, the tempo gradually but relentlessly rising to a crescendo. He is surprised that he remembers it; his grandmother died when he was ten and he is sure he hasn't heard the music since. He turns up the volume, and the melancholy music fills the van.

She used to visit them once a year for two weeks. He always suspected that he was her favourite grandchild, maybe because he bore the closest resemblance to his father, her eldest son. Some nights he was allowed to sleep with her in the double bed in the guest room. On school nights he would have to be in bed by eight, but before lights-out she would read him a story from the Bible. Sometimes her light snoring would wake him during the night. Then he would listen to the doves cooing softly in the nooks of the thatch roof, before falling asleep again.

The piece appears even sadder now and he feels detached from himself. For a minute or so it seems he can see, grasp, the past, his past, not just as disjointed fragments of memory but as a coherent whole: the long years of school; cycling before dawn through the quiet suburbs of Pretoria with his bag of newspapers; exchanging a school uniform for another uniform; black workers toyi-toying at the University of Cape Town; the tedium of putting on a suit and trading bonds; the hearing and the questions. And Louise, always Louise.

11

When he walks past the Sturgeon house the next evening Monica is playing a ball game with an exuberant fair-headed boy in the brightly lit driveway. She notices him and takes the boy by the hand and walks towards him. He tightens his grip on Rex's leash.

'Hallo,' she says. Her skin glows and her hair is damp, as if she has just got out of a bath. She looks down at the boy. 'This is Michael. Say hallo to the nice man, Michael.'

The boy looks up at him. 'Are you a policeman?'

'Something like that,' he says, smiling.

Before he can stop him, the boy has reached out and strokes Rex's head. 'Don't do that, he's not used to children,' he says. But Rex licks the small hand eagerly.

Monica pushes her hair back. 'I want to come talk to you last night, but Mr and Mrs Sturgeon go out – I look after Michael.' Her eyes are blue, a pale and clear blue.

'How are you feeling now?' he asks.

'Very good, thank you very much.'

There is an awkward silence while he thinks of what to say next. But she speaks first. 'Where you from?'

He smiles. Even to a foreigner it is apparent that he does not hail from here. 'South Africa.' Although he knows the answer, he asks, 'And you?'

'I am from Czech Republic.' She has a way of leaning her head slightly to one side when she talks.

'And how are you finding London?'

She nods her head. 'Is good, is good, but very expensive. Why you come to London?'

To run away, to find my wife, to decide what I'm going to do with the rest of my life. He says, 'To earn some money, and then to travel in Europe.'

'Then you must see Prague. I will show you!' she laughs. Her teeth are small and white.

Michael tugs her hand. 'I'm hungry.'

She shrugs and winks at him. 'Okay. It is nice talking to you.'

It is Sunday, his day off. The house is back at full complement: Chris and JB returned earlier in the day on the overnight flight from Johannesburg,

Marius the day before. All three are tanned, and everyone sits at the kitchen table. Rain streams down the kitchen window while they tell Steve and him about their holidays.

Marius says, 'It's depressing to be back in this shithole. And they gave me a lot of shit at Heathrow yesterday.'

'How come?' asks Chris.

Marius snorts. 'The Immigration guys took me away for questioning when they saw I had only three weeks left on my youth visa. And in came this bitch who wanted to know why I was coming back for such a short while. Took me an hour to convince her that I was just coming back to pack up my stuff.'

'So what you're going to do next time – come through Ireland?' asks JB.

He has heard of this backdoor route, which was used by South Africans who had overstayed their visas. They flew from Europe to Dublin on one of the low-cost carriers, knowing that the Irish immigration officials did not ask many questions. And from Ireland one could travel to the UK on a ferry without one's passport being checked again.

'Don't know. I'll double-cross that bridge when I get there,' says Marius, grinning. 'Maybe I'll have to lose my passport again and get a fresh one.'

Steve lights a cigarette and asks, 'So anyway, how was it?'

Marius stretches out and intertwines his fingers behind his head. 'Great. Played golf, braaivleis, chicks, the full monty. And New Year, man, we had a lekker time in Plett – I scored twice.'

He listens with half an ear to Marius, who is already balding at twenty-three, and – for all the tales of the girls he has impregnated – has never been seen with a girl by anyone in the house. As for his own New Year: he had walked with Rex to Hampstead Heath just before midnight, and had watched, from the observation point near Kenwood House, fireworks exploding over London, lighting up the sky like tracer fire and illumination flares.

'Ja, South Africa's still the best country in the world,' Chris says. 'Just a pity that the baboons are now running the zoo.'

Steve says, 'Live and make your money here, go on holiday there, and …'

JB dives in. 'Easy for you to say, you fucking Pom, with a British passport in the back pocket! Real fucking soutpiel, one foot in South

Africa, one foot here, cock hanging in the sea in the middle.' The others laugh at the hackneyed joke.

Steve blows smoke in his direction. 'Don't be jealous now, just because you fucking Japies are too stupid to look after yourselves.'

Chris says, 'People there are pretty depressed at the moment – you know, crime, affirmative action, those things. And then there's all this Truth and Reconciliation bullshit – my father says it's just another way of making us feel guilty, to get us to accept whatever is dished out to us without complaining.'

The reference to the TRC reminds him of his amnesty application. In an office somewhere, it is awaiting a ruling. Perhaps it has already been judged, the verdict given.

'Fuck politics,' says Marius. 'I'm not interested. Anyway, the fight's over now, and we lost. If you want to live in South Africa, you must accept that it's a black country on a black continent, finish and klaar, no going back. And if you can't accept that, get the fuck out of there and go live somewhere else.'

Chris splutters. 'I'm accepting fuck all! Who says it's only a black country? It's my country too – my family tree goes back more than three hundred years.'

'So what're you doing here?' asks Marius.

'Same as you,' Chris responds.

'What do you think, Paul?' asks Steve.

All of them look at him. 'Think about what?' he says.

'The New South Africa,' says Steve.

What to say to them? They were not yet born when Soweto erupted, were at primary school when the Border War ended, in high school at the time of the 1994 elections.

'At least there is a new South Africa,' he says. 'Ten years ago a lot of people thought that it would never happen, that there would be civil war and bloodshed.'

'But what about all the crime and so on?' Chris asks, frowning.

'I think things will maybe get worse before they get better.' He sees that the answer does not satisfy them. Maybe violence was in the genes of his country, he thinks. In the eighteenth century the black tribes and the white settlers in the Eastern Cape had fought over land and cattle for nearly a hundred years; in the nineteenth century Shaka's decimation and dispersion of the other black tribes had created the vacuum in the

Free State and Transvaal that the Voortrekkers had quickly filled; in the twentieth century the British Empire and the Boers had in turn battled over the same territory. What was the difference between a cattle raid on an Eastern Cape farm two hundred years ago and a Limpopo farm attack today? The same eternal struggle, between those who had and those who did not, but in South Africa fought on a more elemental level.

They wait for him to elaborate, but when he remains silent JB says, 'What about a special homecoming zol?'

This time he smokes with them, hungry for the numbness that the dagga will bring. Later he walks out onto the small patch of grass in their back yard. The heavy rain of earlier has subsided to a drizzle. He hears the drone of the perpetual traffic; far above the lights of a plane move across a sky that never darkens completely. On the other side of their rickety wooden fence runs the back of a long row of terraced houses and, here and there, he can see people moving about in kitchens and bedrooms and lounges. He feels the city pressing down on him, all these humans and buildings and cars, a pollution that greys you from the inside.

What is he doing here? Thirty-five years old and a security guard, smoking dagga with youngsters, no closer to finding Louise. And what's to say she is still in London? For all he knows she's gone back to South Africa. In his trouser pocket he fingers her wedding ring. Two months dribbled away in London, with nothing to show for it.

MR VAN VUUREN: Let's now move to the events of the day of the incident and the days after that. Please read paragraphs 18 to 21 into the record.

MR DU TOIT: 'I met Captain Harris on the afternoon of Thursday, 27 November 1987. I briefed him on the status of the project. We agreed to meet again the following afternoon to evaluate the outcome of the project. Thereafter I returned to my residence in Cape Town, where I was alone until the next morning.

'The early news bulletin the next morning reported that a bomb had exploded at a hall in Mitchells Plain, and that there had been an unknown number of fatalities. I was extremely concerned at the report of fatalities. I considered contacting Captain Harris, but decided against this as it was against operational procedures. In any case, even if I had wanted to, I did not know how to get hold of him.

'A later bulletin reported that it was Mr Pretorius and Mr Peters who had been killed in the explosion. The news report said that Mr Pretorius was a senior figure in the ECC, and that Mr Peters was a well-known UDF activist. It was also reported that the police had found what they suspected to be a terrorist arms cache that had been hidden in the hall. I was especially shocked to hear of the death of Mr Pretorius, as I did not know he would be at the meeting.

'That same morning I waited for Tommy from 10h00 to 12h00 in the parking area at Muizenberg beach, but he never showed up. Later that afternoon I met with Captain Harris as arranged. He was extremely disappointed and angry with the outcome of the project. I gave back the remaining R15,000 to Captain Harris.

'When we met a week later, Captain Harris advised me that he had not been able to locate Tommy. We agreed to meet again in February 1987, when the University re-opened after the holidays.'

MR VAN VUUREN: Let's stop there for a moment. Can you describe your state of mind after you heard the news?

MR DU TOIT: I was extremely upset that there had been deaths. I very much regretted this. I knew Mr Pretorius. We had been at high school together. I was also angry that Military Intelligence had used an unprofessional and untrained element such as Tommy. This was not the tradition I had been trained in.

MR VAN VUUREN: Did you not wonder what had happened to Tommy? After all, you still owed him R15,000?

MR DU TOIT: I didn't know what to think. I thought that perhaps he was afraid to face Captain Harris or me in the light of what had happened. Perhaps he knew that he wouldn't be paid as there had been deaths.

MR VAN VUUREN: Thank you. You then deal with your resignation from the South African Defence Force. Will you please read paragraph 22 into the record.

MR DU TOIT: 'During the university holidays in December 1986 and January 1987 I reconsidered my role in the covert action against the ECC. I came to the conclusion that while the objective of combating the enemy on all fronts was correct, I did not want to be involved in actions against civilians. It was the job of the South African Police to maintain internal law and order. I had also now completed my three-year Permanent Force contract. At the end of January 1987 I met with my commanding officer, Colonel Visser, and told him I was not going to renew my Permanent Force contract. He accepted my reasons and I was formally discharged in February 1987.'

MR VAN VUUREN: Thank you. Mr Chairman, that concludes the evidence I want to lead, but before I hand over to my learned colleague Advocate Maubane from Johannesburg for cross-examination, I want to conclude with some final questions to Mr du Toit.

CHAIRPERSON: Please continue.

MR VAN VUUREN: Thank you. Mr du Toit, in these acts that you're asking amnesty for, what were your political objectives?

MR DU TOIT: I believed that at that stage there was a revolutionary onslaught aimed at violently overthrowing the South African Government. The ANC and other organisations were planting bombs in restaurants, necklacing civilians, murdering black policemen and so on. Also, the ANC had subverted civilian organisations like the UDF, ECC and others and were making use of them in their fight against the State. It was a well-known guerrilla tactic - hiding amongst civilians. I was a soldier, a member of the South African Defence Force and I believed that we had to take the fight to them. My actions were driven only by political motives.

MR VAN VUUREN: What do you say to the construction that you were involved in the murder of two unarmed civilians?

MR DU TOIT: I am very sorry for what happened. But that was not the plan, the plan was to frighten and disrupt the ECC, and to make them aware that we knew about them, that we could strike them too. That's why the limpet mine had a remote detonation mechanism, so that it could be exploded at a time when there were no people around. I am also very sorry that we used persons like Tommy.

MR VAN VUUREN: Mr du Toit, do you have anything to say to the families of the victims?

MR DU TOIT: Yes. I want to express my deep regret for their loss. We never wanted to injure or kill anyone. Looking back now, it must be difficult for people to understand why we acted as we did. But at that time we considered it a war, and unfortunately in a war there are sometimes unforeseen casualties. I wish I could change what happened, but I can't.

MR VAN VUUREN: Thank you. And lastly, do you confirm that you have made full disclosure of all relevant facts pertaining to this incident?

MR DU TOIT: I do.

MR VAN VUUREN: Thank you, Mr Chairman.

NO FURTHER QUESTIONS FROM MR VAN VUUREN.

CHAIRPERSON: I think this is a good point to adjourn for lunch. We will reconvene at one-thirty p.m., when Mr Maubane can start his cross-examination.

COMMITTEE ADJOURNS

12

On an overcast afternoon at the end of January he again googles Louise's name on Steve's laptop. To his surprise he gets fifteen thousand hits this time. Then he sees he has spelt her maiden name incorrectly: Smith instead of Smit. On an impulse he decides not to correct the search string but to add 'London' and 'IT' as he usually does; now the search yields only eighty-three references. He scrolls through the web pages, then stops at the results of a London road race: the search engine has highlighted the finishing time of a Louise Smith, a member of the Datagroup IT team. He feels a flicker of excitement. Louise had been an active member of Wanderers Club Road Runners in Johannesburg. He finds the Datagroup website and makes a note of their address and telephone number.

He phones the company and asks for Louise Smith. She called in sick that morning, a secretary informs him. He improvises: could she provide him with Miss Smith's home number? He's from DHL, Miss Smith arranged a shipment with them, he needs to confirm the delivery details. Half an hour later he matches the telephone number with a Kentish Town address on British Telecom's directory enquiry website. He tries to contain his excitement; most likely it will come to nothing. He has to be at work in an hour – he'll follow it up the next day.

As usual, Monica comes out just after nine, after she has put Michael to bed. He watches her walk towards the van. The first time, a few weeks ago, she had knocked on the window of the patrol van and asked if he had a lighter or matches. She wasn't allowed to smoke in the Sturgeon house, she told him. But since then she visits most evenings, spends twenty minutes or so with him in the van, smokes one or two cigarettes. She does most of the talking; he divulges little.

She is in London to improve her English, she has told him, and attends classes at a language college in Finchley Road twice a week. Her sister is a student in Prague, and she is a Robbie Williams fan. She seems uncomplicated and optimistic, effervescent, and he looks forward to the break in the nightly routine.

Monica opens door on the passenger side and gets in. As she takes out a cigarette, she sighs, 'I don't understand these English people.'

He lights her cigarette. 'Trouble with Mrs Sturgeon?'

She puffs out. 'She always complaining – Michael too dirty, wrong clothes, not eating food, always something wrong. And tonight she is angry because I want to go out Friday night – she want to me to work, Mr Sturgeon and she want to go to party. But I tell her I have already make plans, Friday night is my free night.'

He smiles. The first few minutes of their encounters are usually taken up with an update on her stormy relationship with Mrs Sturgeon. Mr Sturgeon, according to her, works long hours at an investment bank in the City and Mrs Sturgeon, other than driving Michael to and from nursery school, spends her days shopping, getting manicures, working out with her personal trainer – and criticising Monica. She is not allowed to use any toilet other than the one next to her loft room, or to swim in the heated basement swimming pool.

A car with its headlights on high beam turns into the street. As it drives past, he vaguely registers three faces turning in their direction, but Monica distracts his attention with a question.

'Sorry, what was that?' he asks.

'What are you doing Friday night?'

'I'm here, working.'

'I think maybe you want to go to club with me and my friend?' She looks away and fiddles with the radio's tuner.

He is surprised. Has she just asked him out? 'With your friend?'

She looks up. 'She is also from Prague. She is au pair in Surrey.'

He laughs. 'A boring old man like me. I'm sure your friend won't be very happy.'

She shakes her head. 'Not so old, not so boring.'

She is serious, he realises. 'That's nice of you, but I have to work on Friday.'

She presses his forearm. 'Okay. But next time, no excuse.'

He is surprised to feel a quickening. She is attractive, no doubt about that.

'How long you still going to be in London?' she asks.

'I don't know, three, four months maybe.'

She smiles. 'Four months, I hope.' Then she asks, 'And South Africa now, how is it now?'

He shrugs. 'Like any other country, good things, bad things.'

'But before, it was bad, not?' She frowns. 'Apartheid, it was bad for the black people in South Africa?'

Apartheid, his language's most famous offspring, a word that will perhaps outlive the tongue that gave birth to it, he thinks. And how to answer, how to summarise a complex tale? But a summary is all that people have time for; the world has many stories.

'Yes, it was.' Suddenly he feels defensive. 'But there are many other countries in Africa where it was, and still is, bad for black people.'

She nods. 'I don't know much about Africa.'

Later, after she has gone home, he thinks of Lina, the Zulu woman who had worked for his parents for thirty years, from before his birth, and who also wasn't permitted to use their swimming pool or the house toilets. He probably saw more of her than his own mother when he was growing up. What is certain is that she had spent more time with his brother and him than with her own three children, who lived with their grandmother in Mamelodi. In the mornings Lina made breakfast for Pieter and him; in the afternoons she had lunch ready when they returned from school or sports practice; in the evenings she looked after them when their parents went out. She knew where he hid his cigarettes, what he and his friends did when his parents weren't there.

He remembers that the first time he came home on army leave, Lina was waiting for him in the kitchen, obviously happy to see him. There was an awkward moment when he stepped forward to greet her and wondered if should kiss her as he had his mother. But he had never kissed a black person before; in the event, he greeted her with a handshake. It has been ten years since he last saw her; she had retired to her birth-place somewhere in KwaZulu-Natal when he was at university. He only heard about it later, and he had never had the chance to say goodbye. And what Lina really thought about things he never knew. But that's not true, he remembers; one morning Lina's mask had slipped.

That morning his ears burned and his eyes teared as he cycled with his newspapers through the quiet streets on his new ten-speed Raleigh bicycle, his thirteenth-birthday present. Their suburb straddled a koppie; sometimes he had to stand upright on the bike's pedals to get up a hill. It was one of Pretoria's wealthier suburbs, with large, double-storey houses on one-acre properties, some with tennis courts, all with pools. Most of the year the gardens were lush, flourishing in the sub-tropical temperature and carefully tended by black garden boys. But it was winter and the jacaranda trees that lined the streets were bare and frost covered the lawns.

He had cycled past a rubbish truck with a dozen black dustmen hanging from the back and running alongside. The men were dressed in blue overalls and had tied white and red handkerchiefs around their heads; despite the cold most of them had pulled down the tops of their overalls and tied the sleeves around their waists. The men took turns to jump down and feed the dustbins left out on the pavements into the metal jaws of the truck. They exhaled bursts of steam as they jogged to and fro next to the slowly moving truck, laughing and chanting while they worked. Every now and then their foreman gave a piercing whistle to hurry them on. Once again he noticed how well built they were: not an ounce of fat, every muscle perfectly defined. They reminded him of the pictures of Zulu impis in his Standard Six history textbook, the same impis that had killed hundreds of Voortrekker women and children in Natal at a place that had been renamed Weenen, the Dutch word for weeping.

He pulled up next to a battery-powered milk van, stretched out his arm and leaned against the door. 'Hallo, Isaac, how are you this morning?'

The driver, an old black man wearing a battered Salvation Army cap, raised his hand by way of greeting. He listened patiently as Isaac recited his usual litany of woes: his bad back, the struggle to get together the lobola for his youngest son's prospective father-in-law, township tsotsis who had tried to rob his wife.

'I better get going, otherwise I'm going to be late for school,' he said when Isaac eventually finished. But he didn't push himself away from the van.

Isaac winked. 'I have no eyes in the back of my head, have I?'

He smiled, reversed his bicycle a yard, and lifted a bottle of milk out of a plastic crate.

'Thanks, Isaac,' he said. 'See you tomorrow. Hamba Khale.'

He watched as Isaac, regally at the helm with his cap jutting out a nautical angle, navigated his vessel down the street and disappeared around the bend.

With his thumb he punched a hole in the foil cap of the bottle. But as he lifted the bottle to his mouth he saw three black men sprint towards him; on the tarmac the milk bottle shattered. Then a yellow police van roared into view, its tyres squealing as it rounded the bend. The men ran past him, eyes white and breathing hard, like the horses on the farm after a stiff gallop. He turned around. The men had split up: one ran towards a garden wall, the other two made for the open veld that bordered the street. The police van slid to a stop; its back doors had swung open and an Alsatian tumbled out, followed by two black policemen in tight-fitting blue uniforms and shiny black shoes. The snarling dog skidded on the icy grass but immediately found its footing and gave chase. In three or four bounds it caught up with the man trying to pull himself over the wall, jumped up and sank its teeth into his shoulder. The man screamed and dog and human fell back onto the grass. The two policemen reached them; one pulled the dog away while the other handcuffed and then bundled the moaning man, on whose torn shirt a red stain was already blooming, into the back of the van. A few seconds later the street was deserted again, a dull smudge on the grass the only evidence of the recent struggle.

His legs trembled at he raced home. He went into the kitchen through the back door. Around the kitchen table were his family: Pieter, ten years old, in his red school uniform; his mother in a blue dressing gown; his father in a three-piece suit, paging through the *Oggendblad*. Lina was washing a frying pan in the sink.

He sat down and breathlessly told them what had happened. But his father seemed irritated with this disruption of his morning routine; Pieter carried on eating his Weet-Bix; only his mother was interested. While he was talking he started to feel embarrassed: the story was coming out all wrong and sounded inconsequential.

When he was through, he asked, 'Why do you think they were running away from the police, Pa?' Even though Lina stood with her back towards them, he noticed that she had stopped scrubbing.

'They probably didn't have passes,' his father said, raising his newspaper and concealing his face once again. His mother frowned as Lina banged a saucepan in the sink.

He nodded at the newspaper. 'Ja, I suppose Pa is right.' A year or two ago his father had explained it: the Xhosas, Zulus, Sothos, Vendas and a half dozen or so other tribes had their own countries – homelands they were called – where they lived. To visit and work in South Africa they needed a pass, which was a kind of passport; many of them tried to come to South Africa without their passports.

His father again lowered his newspaper and frowned. 'Lina, what's going on in Soweto? Why are your people making trouble again?'

With her back still towards the table, Lina said, 'No, baas, I don't know anything about those things.'

His mother glanced at his father. 'Should he really be delivering newspapers at a time like this?'

His father touched his lips with a paper serviette. 'Nonsense. The police have everything under control.' He saw from the way his mother pursed her lips together that she wasn't satisfied with his father's reply.

'But is this a time to be taking chances?' she persisted. His father flushed and looked up again. He felt his stomach tighten. Pieter kept his eyes fixed on his bowl.

'Don't you think I know what I'm talking about?' his father said.

'Don't worry, Ma, I'll be careful,' he said quickly. She gave him a hurt look, stood up and walked to the fridge. His father carried on reading his newspaper.

The kitchen door slammed when Lina went outside. His mother sighed. 'How many times have I told her not to do that? They're just like children sometimes.'

Later in the morning he dozes off in the van. But in the last moment before sleep a thought at the edge of his consciousness prods him awake – the car that drove past him and Monica earlier in the evening. A white saloon, a Ford or Toyota maybe, and three faces. He had seen them for only a split second. He closes his eyes and concentrates. Two faces are indistinct, but he something bothers him about the third one, that of the man in the front passenger seat. Something had covered part of the man's face. Then he remembers – it was an orthopaedic nose-guard.

13

He watches the front door of the house in Kentish Town from a phone booth across the road, about thirty metres farther along. It is half-past seven in the morning; he has come straight from work to the address he noted down the previous day. The street is a cul-de-sac, lined with large, somewhat run-down houses, three- and four-storey buildings set back a few yards from the pavement. The street must have seen grander times; it looks as if the houses had once been individual residences, but now most have two front doors, and next to the doors there are rows of buzzers. In the past hour the front door of the house he is watching has opened only once, to let out an old man with a poodle who walked off towards the High Street. Everything drips; it had rained hard the previous night.

He is busy lighting a cigarette when the door opens again. A woman comes out. At first he is not sure. At this distance and through the fogged up glass of the booth her features are indistinct. But when she flicks her hair back in that distinctive way as she turns in his direction he recognises her. He drops the cigarette. He struggles to breathe; it is as if a great hand is squeezing his chest. He turns sideways, backs up against the scores of business cards of various big-breasted prostitutes which are pasted against the side of the booth, and lifts the cold receiver to his ear. The familiar sensations of spotting a surveillance target: the slowing of time, apprehension and excitement mingled, senses heightened. She walks down the steps to the street gate, stops, slides her bag from her shoulder, reaches inside and lifts a cigarette to her mouth. The flame flickers around the tip and smoke rises into the damp, spongy sky.

She walks briskly over the soggy layer of brown leaves glued to the pavement. He watches her from the corner of his eye, his back turned towards her side of the street. She is wearing an oversize jersey, leather boots and a long skirt. As she draws level with him on the other side of the street she moves out of sight. Afraid of attracting her attention, he doesn't turn around at once. When he does, she has reached the High Street and is walking in the direction of the tube station.

He grins and bunches his fists, he wants to shout out and punch the air. But he waits fifteen minutes before leaving the booth, in case she has forgotten something and returns. He stays on the opposite side of the street and walks towards her house. His knee is stiff from the long wait in the booth. The house has three storeys, stairs leading down to a basement, no burglar bars, and large sliding windows on each floor. He walks to the end of the cul-de-sac before crossing the street and doubling back.

In front of the house he stops and lights a cigarette. The front door has a double lock. From where he stands he cannot read the nameplates next to the buzzers. He looks up. A curtain twitches – someone on the third floor is watching him. He slips his cigarette packet and lighter into his anorak pocket and slowly walks away.

He decides to walk home. He gets claustrophobic in the crowded carriages and the dirty tunnels of the Underground, and he needs to think. But his thoughts are disordered; he feels light-footed, elated, confused, and walks without noticing anything around him.

She seems to have settled in well – a permanent job, athletics, probably friends from running and work. What had he missed before her flight? Surely all this had not just happened on the spur of the moment?

After a kilometre or so the screaming and shouting of children break into his thoughts. Across the road, on a tarmac playground behind high railings, schoolchildren are milling about, scruffy boys kicking balls to and fro, gossiping girls in small groups. Not that different from his high school. Before school and during breaks they had also congregated in a tarmac quadrangle bordered by red-brick classrooms, the boys clustered on one side, the girls on the other, in the middle a few brave couples. It was André who, on the first day of their Matric year, had noticed the new girl. 'Paul, look there. Not bad, hey? Wonder who she is?' They found out in the first class – a double English session – when Mrs Mennie introduced the new girl from Cape Town. Louise hadn't flinched under the thirty pairs of eyes scrutinising her, and had looked back at them challengingly.

He has found her. Now what? Before he can take the next step he needs to find out more, he decides. Does she live with anyone, what does she do apart from work, who are her friends? Thorough reconnaissance is the key to any mission's success.

In Euston Road he goes into a fast food restaurant and orders a doner kebab and bottle of water. While he waits in the queue a group of youths, Asian or maybe Arab, outfitted in low-slung trousers, baseball caps and expensive trainers, come into the shop and line up behind him. When he gets his order he turns around and squeezes past them. The largest one looks annoyed and says, 'Hey, brother, who you pushing?' He stops and sizes them up. It would be easy. But he turns around and walks away. As leaves the premises he hears them laughing.

He goes to bed when he gets home. But he is too agitated to sleep, and gets up at noon. He opens his *London A-Z* and plots a travel route to Datagroup's offices.

He takes the tube to Hatton Cross in West London, from there a bus. His fellow passengers are housewives with shopping bags, pensioners and noisy schoolchildren. The bus winds its way through suburbs with straggly trees and bland houses. Twenty minutes later the bus stops outside an office park; on the other side of a man-made lake he sees a large Datagroup sign.

A seated security guard watches him from a booth as he walks through the entrance to the park. But he knows – walk purposefully, don't look at him. Dishevelled ducks bob on the murky water of the lake. Around its perimeter three- and four-storey buildings glitter like shards of glass. He feels exposed: Louise could be watching him at this very moment. As he walks on the path along the side of the lake he tries to identify a suitable observation post. Here and there along the path are benches, but a solitary sitter on a cold January afternoon would attract attention. At the far end of the park is a bus shelter, but it is too far from the Datagroup building. The rest of the terrain is just as unpromising: a service road that circles the lake, exposed areas between the buildings, an open-air parking lot behind them.

He sees two men walking from the parking lot and slows down. When they walk up the steps of the building next to Datagroup, he is hard on their heels. They walk past an elderly security guard behind a marble counter and the visitors' register towards the bank of lifts. The guard looks at him. He nods in the direction of the men and carries on walking. He steps into the lift after the men and pushes the button above the one already lit. On the third floor he exits. On either side of the lifts are receptionists behind glass doors and, on the left, a stairway and a sign for the restrooms. He goes into the men's toilets.

His luck holds: it is a perfect observation point. When he opens the window in the furthest cubicle he can see the side of Datagroup's building, which – unlike its façade – is clad in transparent glass. The offices are open plan, people and workstations visible everywhere. He sits down, then carefully scans and rescans each of building's four floors. How did Louise end up here? How was she coping in this alien environment?

He is not quite sure what exactly Datagroup does; according to its website it provides application services and web hosting, whatever that may be. He finds the jargon of the IT industry impenetrable, the business models of IT companies opaque. These days anything to do with technology seems to be a licence to print money, and every week the NASDAQ reached new highs. Louise had often urged him to buy some IT shares, but he had never got around to it. Even though he had spent the greater part of his waking life trading bonds, he had never been particularly interested in the financial markets; it had been a job, like any other purposeless job, that was all.

And he had also never quite managed to throw himself wholeheartedly, like most of his peers, into the relentless accumulation of money and possessions – a handicap that Louise ascribed to a deplorable lack of ambition. But capitalism is just another ideology with its own rigid dogma and false promises, he thinks, and of that he has had his fill.

Two hours later he sees her. She is smoking and talking to a woman outside the entrance to the Datagroup building. Once again he feels the elation of earlier that day. After a minute or so she turns and looks in his direction, as if she senses that she is being watched. He pulls back from the window. But she can't possibly see him, he realises: he is watching her through an inch-wide gap four storeys above her. Then she and the woman stub out their cigarettes and go back into the building, disappearing from view but reappearing a few seconds later when they walk through the lobby towards the lifts. They emerge on the second floor. Now, as she sits down behind a partition, he realises why he hadn't been able to spot her earlier. He watches for another forty minutes, then leaves for work.

14

After work the next morning he returns to Kentish Town; hopefully she doesn't work on Saturdays. He is bone tired, and dozes as the train shudders through the tunnels. He wakes up at Tufnell Park, the station after hers. He decides to walk back to Kentish Town along the High Street. Plastic bags, crumpled hamburger boxes and cigarette butts litter the kerb. The high streets of London's suburbs seem interchangeable: betting shops, off-licences, estate agents, coffee shops, fast-food restaurants cheek by jowl.

Near Louise's house he criss-crosses Kentish Town's high street several times before he makes up his mind. The observation point will have to be McDonald's: from there he can see the tube station and the junction where her street joins the High Street. He goes inside, buys breakfast and sits at a table at the window.

Three hours later, distracted by a cleaner bustling around the table, he nearly misses her. When he looks up, he sees her in the High Street near the entrance to the tube station. He quickly goes out and walks along the opposite side of the street. When she goes into the station he jogs through the traffic and reaches the entrance just as she is going through the gates at the top of the escalators. He follows her down the escalator but waits for a train to arrive before he ventures out on to the platform. He is just in time to see her step into a carriage, and gets into an adjoining one. Through the windows of the connecting doors he can see her back. It is a short journey, for she disembarks at the next station, Camden Town.

Coming out of the station he walks into a crowd of people on the pavement. For a few seconds he fears that he has lost the trail, but then he sees the back of her head twenty yards from him. It is easy to conceal himself in the crowd, and he manages to keep a distance of half a block between them. He follows her past scores of dingy shops and a large open-air flea market. The sun has come out and the sky is a crisp blue, but the air is cold and smells of stale vomit and rotting vegetables. She walks over a small bridge that spans an oily canal, then turns into a large market complex – Camden Lock, the overhead sign reads.

She goes into a restaurant overlooking the canal. He walks into a second-hand-bookshop that faces the restaurant from across a narrow lock. For the next hour he flips through books he selects at random, always keeping an eye on the restaurant's entrance. The caftaned manager glances at him from time to time, but she leaves him alone.

Then Louise reappears. This time she is holding hands with a dark-haired man in an overcoat.

'Is there a problem?' the manager asks.

He turns to the woman, only then sees the paperback book crumpled in his hands. 'I'm sorry,' he says, straightening the book and replacing it on the shelf.

His heart races as he follows them through the market complex. Every minute brings a new, and painful, revelation: Louise ruffling her companion's hair, laughing at something he says, pulling him by the hand to show him a jacket. Her companion is older and shorter than he is, early forties at a rough guess. A sharp dresser – leather shoes, corduroy trousers, expensive coat and haircut. He is slenderly built and looks fit and light on his feet. A fellow runner perhaps?

He tries to focus on following them without being detected; he is not yet ready to think about the implications of what he is seeing. Somehow time passes, and by mid-afternoon he is back in Kentish Town, watching them go into her house. He lights a cigarette but gags when he inhales the smoke.

He walks to the front door of the house and reads the nameplates next to the intercom – L Smith lives on the top floor. From across the street he watches – the top two windows are lit and, occasionally, he sees indistinct figures moving behind the curtains. At five he phones Jim, the duty supervisor, and reports sick.

Another hour passes, but they do not come out again. He is tormented by visions of Louise in bed, her legs jackknifed around the man, teeth bared and eyes closed, or on her knees, being mounted from behind. His chest hurts. Later he climbs over the gate at the side of the house to see if he can find a way up to the third floor. But there are no stairs, and the drainpipes are too far from the windows.

Then it starts raining and he takes shelter in the phone booth down the road. Unable to see anything from the booth, he returns to his position across the street from the house. He is quickly soaked to the skin, his feet squishing in his shoes. It is nothing, he tells himself, he is used to worse – once, hiding from the patrols hunting them, he and another operator lay for two days in several inches of water in a shona. But the years behind a computer terminal have made him soft and he has to clench his jaw muscles to stop his teeth from chattering. At half-past ten the lights on the third floor go off – her companion is clearly staying the night.

At midnight he walks back to the tube station. The carriage fills with drunken Saturday night revellers who fall against him when the train grinds to a halt, or push him aside when they get on or off. He allows himself to be buffeted; in this city, at this time, who is he to complain?

At home everyone is asleep. He dries himself and zips himself into his sleeping bag. But he can't stop shivering, and spasms of pain pulse through his head.

He dreams of a room with a locked door – inside are Louise and André. He beats his fist against the wood, but nobody opens. He shouts, but they don't seem to hear.

'Paul, Paul, wake up!' He blinks in the sharp light. Steve is shaking him by his shoulder; behind him stand Chris, Marius and JB.

'Jesus, man, are you okay? What's going on? You were screaming your head off,' Steve says.

He raises himself on his elbows.

Steve frowns. 'You're sweating like a pig, what's wrong with you?'

'Flu,' he says. His body aches, his eyes feel swollen.

'Do you want a Panado or something?'

He nods.

Chris brings him a tumbler of water and two tablets. 'Please don't scream like that again, I nearly had a heart attack.'

He swallows the pills and falls back on the bed.

When he wakes it is light outside. His headache has shrunk to a dull throb, but his throat burns and he is stiff, as stiff as he used to feel the morning after a hard rugby game at school. It is Sunday, his free day, so at least he can rest. He closes his eyes again. Outside, in the street, a woman is talking to someone, children's voices drift from the direction of the park. From downstairs he hears the murmur of voices, a television perhaps.

But the lull is brief – images of Louise and her boyfriend soon assail him again. He gets up, pulls on a tracksuit and goes to the bathroom. His urine is colourless and gives off an acrid smell.

In the lounge Steve and Chris are watching a France–England rugby international, the Sunday papers spread out on the carpet in front of them.

Steve lifts his hand. 'Howzit. Feeling better?'

He nods.

'Jesus, you had us worried last night,' Chris says.

'Sorry.'

Steve lights a cigarette. 'You better make peace with this André guy, whoever he is. He's really bugging you.'

He frowns as though puzzled. 'André? Don't know any André.'

'Okay, if you say so, but you sure were shouting his name last night,' Steve says.

He goes to the kitchen and mixes milk and cornflakes in a bowl. But when he lifts the spoon to his mouth the smell of the milk makes him nauseous. It is too much; he wants numbness.

He walks to the off-licence on the corner. The sun is out, but the air is damp and musty, like that in a dark cellar. He returns with a bottle of whisky. Steve and Chris are still engrossed in the game and don't notice when he walks past the lounge. In his room he gags on the first mouthful, but manages to swallow it down. The second goes down easier.

After the fourth glass he feels a surge of confidence. Now he can think of her without a tightness gripping his throat and a hollowness in the pit of his stomach. Maybe there is still hope. After all, how long could she have been seeing this man? She's only been in London for a short while, three and a half months maximum. But then again, the flame always burns the strongest at the start. The long nights of lying awake and longing for her, the months of searching, the continuous anxiety: a waste of time.

As he drinks more, he becomes angry. It would be easy – follow his rival, wait for the right moment, then frighten him badly, warn him off. For a while his plans of retaliation bring solace. But he knows he is merely fantasising. Louise would probably get to hear of it, and that would kill any chance he had. That is if he had any.

He pours another glass, drinks it quickly. Suddenly he has to go. He vomits into the toilet until his neck muscles ache and his forehead is clammy. Afterwards he rests his cheek against the cool rim of the basin. When he gets up from his knees, Steve and Chris are watching him from the doorway.

'For fuck's sake, what's wrong with you? Chris asks.

Steve glances into his room, sees the near empty bottle. 'Looks like he's done some serious damage to a lot of whisky.'

He pushes past them and falls onto his bed. They follow him into the room. He turns towards the wall and closes his eyes. They are still talking to him but he feels himself slipping away.

ON RESUMPTION: CROSS-EXAMINATION BY ADVOCATE MAUBANE

CHAIRPERSON: Is everyone present? Good. Mr Maubane, you may start your cross-examination

MR MAUBANE: Thank you, Chairperson. Mr du Toit, that apology of yours was very moving. But I put it to you that you are applying for amnesty only because you knew you were going to be exposed, and because you feared prosecution.

MR VAN VUUREN: Mr Chairman, I must object. As we all know, the motives of an applicant in applying for amnesty are not relevant.

CHAIRPERSON: Mr Maubane, please restrict your questioning to the matter at hand.

MR MAUBANE: Yes, Chairperson. Mr du Toit, is this the first time you have apologised to the family members of the victims?

MR DU TOIT (still under oath): Yes.

MR MAUBANE: So you waited thirteen years before making your eloquent apology? You ... (intervention)

MR VAN VUUREN: Mr Chairman, I must ...

CHAIRPERSON: Yes, yes. Mr Maubane, please.

MR MAUBANE: Yes, Chairperson. Mr du Toit, you are aware that in terms of the Reconciliation Act you can only be granted amnesty provided that you make full disclosure of all the relevant facts, and also provided that you demonstrate that your actions were motivated by political objectives?

MR DU TOIT: Yes.

MR MAUBANE: Good. Now, this morning you said that these killings were not the first you had been involved in. What other killings had you been involved in?

MR DU TOIT: They were related to my military service.

MR MAUBANE: How many killings were there? Did any happen inside the borders of this country?

MR DU TOIT: You have my application. I am not applying for any other incidents.

MR MAUBANE: But you had killed before, this was not your first time?

MR DU TOIT: No.

MR MAUBANE: So can we take it that killing and murder were a routine matter for you? ... (intervention)

MR VAN VUUREN: Mr Chairman, I must now object. My client has applied for amnesty for the incident in question, not for any other alleged incidents.

MR MAUBANE: Chairperson, my line of questioning goes to the heart of this matter. I intend to show that the deaths of Mr Peters and Mr Pretorius were not accidental but premeditated, and that Mr du Toit was selected for this operation because he was trained in killing.

CHAIRPERSON: I will allow. Please continue, Mr Maubane.

MR MAUBANE: So you killed as a matter of routine.

MR DU TOIT: I was a soldier, it was a war. I followed orders.

MR MAUBANE: But what kind of soldier makes war on unarmed civilians?

MR DU TOIT: The war had changed. The ANC had brought the war into the townships and cities, they were the ones using civilians.

MR MAUBANE: Is it not so that in the Special Forces you and your colleagues received training in assassination techniques?

MR DU TOIT: We received training in all kinds of things.

MR MAUBANE: Please answer the question.

MR DU TOIT: All Special Forces units, everywhere in the world, receive training in the covert elimination of enemies. Our training was no different.

MR MAUBANE: And did your training include instruction in the use of explosives?

MR DU TOIT: Yes, we all received instruction in this.

MR MAUBANE: Mr du Toit, you are being very modest. Didn't you in fact undergo specialised demolitions training, something only certain Special Forces members undergo?

MR DU TOIT: I did attend additional courses, that is correct.

MR MAUBANE: And don't you consider that to be a relevant fact that should have been included in your application?

MR DU TOIT: I don't understand.

MR MAUBANE: I think you do. Mr Peters and Mr Pretorius were killed in an explosion. You were trained in explosives. Don't you see any connection?

MR DU TOIT: I don't see the relevance. Showing someone how to use a remote detonation device does not require any special training. Anyone can do that.

MR MAUBANE: I put it to you that your specialised training is why you were chosen for undercover work.

MR DU TOIT: As I said in my application, because of my knee injury I was no longer fit for active duty.

MR MAUBANE: Mr du Toit, I put it to you that at the time you were seconded to Military Intelligence, a decision had already been taken to assassinate members of the anti-apartheid movement, and that is why you, a trained killer and demolitions expert, were chosen.

MR DU TOIT: You may choose to believe that, but you are wrong. And I object to being called a killer. I was a soldier.

MR MAUBANE: Come now, why so sensitive? You yourself have admitted to killings.

MR VAN VUUREN: Mr Chairman, these snide remarks are uncalled for. My client has admitted to being involved in the accidental deaths of Mr Pretorius and Mr Peters. But to be called a killer is unfair. By that standard any soldier can be called a trained killer.

CHAIRPERSON: Mr Maubane, you will refrain from using the term 'trained killer'.

MR MAUBANE: Mr du Toit, did you know of any other undercover Military Intelligence agents operating at the University of Cape Town while you were a student there?

MR DU TOIT: Yes, there were others.

MR MAUBANE: How many were there?

MR DU TOIT: A couple, I can't recall how many.

MR MAUBANE: Did you work with them?

MR DU TOIT: I did from time to time.

MR MAUBANE: Were they also from Special Forces or from the Defence Force?

MR DU TOIT: No, they were ordinary students.

MR MAUBANE: Who did they report to?

MR DU TOIT: To me.

MR MAUBANE: They reported to you, but you can't recall how many there were? I find that very strange. What were their names?

MR DU TOIT: I prefer not to answer that question. They were not involved in this incident.

MR MAUBANE: So you refuse to disclose their names to this Commission.

MR DU TOIT: That is so.

MR MAUBANE: And are you of the opinion that you are disclosing all relevant facts as you are expected to do?

MR DU TOIT: I do not consider their names to be a relevant fact.

MR MAUBANE: Well, we'll leave that for the Commission to decide. This morning you said that psychological warfare included damaging the cars of the organisers of the ECC. What other operations against the ECC were you involved in during your time at UCT?

MR DU TOIT: I am not applying for amnesty for other incidents.

MR MAUBANE: Mr du Toit, were you or were you not involved in other operations aimed at destabilising the ECC?

MR DU TOIT: I am not applying for amnesty for any other incidents.

MR MAUBANE: Your attitude is most unhelpful. You are expected to disclose all relevant facts, which include your activities as a Military Intelligence agent during the period leading up to the killing of Mr Peters and Mr Pretorius.

MR DU TOIT: That is your opinion, you are entitled to it. I disagree.

MR MAUBANE: I see. Mr du Toit, you seem quite proud of your service in the Special Forces. Am I correct?

MR DU TOIT: I have nothing to be ashamed of, if that's what you're getting at.

15

Rex wags his tail and scrabbles at the wire door of his cage when he walks into the kennels. The dog jumps up against him and licks his hand when he unlocks the gate. Irritably he pushes him away; he is still hung over. The Alsatian drops his tail and looks at him mournfully. He immediately feels guilty and scratches him behind the ears; he has taken an unexpected liking to Rex.

The traffic on the North Circular crawls. It is raining softly, a fine sleet, and the ash-grey sky hangs low. On his left are shabby warehouses and low office buildings, on his right a row of terraced houses whose front doors are only twenty feet from the busy road. How do their occupants endure the perpetual droning of the cars and trucks, the exhaust fumes, the vibrating windows? Sometimes he feels dwarfed by the immensity of this city, a piece of driftwood floating in this ocean of people, people who lead nondescript lives behind the walls of anonymous houses and flats.

It had seemed to him that finding Louise would be the trigger for a fresh start. But now everything has changed. She has also crossed a border, and the knowledge tugs at him, weighs him down. He is immobilised, he realises, not only in place but also in time, unable to move backward or forward.

That evening when Monica gets into the van she says, 'Paul, what's wrong? You don't look so good.'

'I've been ill. Flu.'

'Mrs Sturgeon and Michael also, they are both in bed. But you must get better, we must go out on Friday night.' She slips her hand into her coat pocket and produces two tickets. 'Is for theatre. From Mr Sturgeon, they can't go.'

'Monica, I have to work.'

She examines him sideways. 'You don't want to go with me?'

'No, it's not that. I was sick on Saturday, I can't take another night off this week.'

She folds her arms. 'But you said you could change with colleague.'

He does not have enough energy to argue with her. 'Look, I'll see what I can do,' he says.

She smiles. 'Is going to be very good. Is famous play by Arthur Miller.'

He's never heard of Arthur Miller, but then again, he has been in a theatre only a couple of times in his life. 'I didn't know you were a theatre-goer.'

'Of course. We have more than fifty theatres in Prague. My father take us often. Even the president of our country write plays.'

From their conversations over the past few weeks he has gleaned bits and pieces about Monica's background: a deceased father, a mother and two siblings in Prague, a psychology degree from a Czech university. He has only a vague idea of where exactly the Czech Republic – which he incorrectly called Czechoslovakia, as Monica was quick to point out – is located in Europe. His only previous contact with her country was in the form of an automatic rifle he took off the body of a Cuban lieutenant outside Cuvelai. The letters BRNO were engraved on the rifle; according to the armourer at Fort Rev it was the name of a Czech town with a famous weapons factory.

He watches her light a cigarette. She is the opposite of Louise: dark, small; more girl than woman. She is only eight years younger than him, but she is of a different generation. What does she want from him?

Later, after midnight, he hits on an idea, and he wonders why he hasn't thought of it before. He checks his map: from Highgate to Kentish Town it is about two miles, fifteen minutes at most with the van.

He parks across the road from her house. From inside the van he watches the windows on the third floor, but they are dark, and all is quiet. Maybe the boyfriend is there, maybe they are snug in bed. He feels empty, as if something is gnawing at his entrails and steadily hollowing him out, a feeling he remembers well. Memory is a curse, he thinks, but now it is here, and he cannot evade it.

He had lunched with Captain Harris in a restaurant in Sea Point. Their lunch ended at three and, afterwards, he drove back to his room in Rondebosch along High Level Road. It was a hot afternoon. Far below Table Bay glittered, and on the horizon he could see Robben Island. He suddenly decided to visit André, whose flat in Tamboerskloof was on his way back.

André's Beetle was in front of the block of flats. But the parking lot was full and he had to drive around the block several times before he found a space. The sun beat down on him as he walked to the flat and through the soles of his sandals he felt the heat of the pavement. He went up to the second floor. It was an old building, probably built in the fifties or sixties, and over the years the floors had been polished to a deep red. André's flat, which he shared with another postgraduate engineering student, was at the end of the corridor. As he approached he heard the nasal strains of Van Morrison's 'Moondance', one of André's favourites. Chick music, André called it: good music to bed a girl to, according to him.

He knocked. Somewhere in the flat he heard muffled voices. But no one came to the door. He knocked again, listened. Van Morrison was reaching a crescendo and the voices had stopped. He smiled. André was on the job, probably with a fresh conquest. Little chance then of him opening the door.

He walked the same way back to his car. But this time he noticed a red Golf parked on the other side of the street. It looked like Louise's, but of course that couldn't be: she was fifty kilometres away in Stellenbosch, why would she be in Cape Town on a week day? As he drew closer he saw that the right side of the back of the car was dented, the same place where Louise had damaged her car when she had backed into a concrete pillar three months ago. He crossed the street and looked inside – a computer science textbook, a folded stack of printouts, a Leonard Cohen cassette tape. The number plates on the front of the car were hers too. Now he realised. He crossed the street without looking; a car hooted and swerved around him.

And he remembers, he remembers what he has avoided thinking of for so long. From where he had concealed himself behind a tree on the other side of the road he had seen them come out on the balcony of André's flat, Louise wrapped in a towel, André bare-chested.

16

The security guard challenges him as he walks towards the lifts. 'Excuse me, sir, where are you going?'

It is the third time he has entered the building next to Datagroup's offices, but the first time that the guard questions him. 'Impact Software.'

'I've seen you around, but are you a visitor or do you work there?'

'Visitor.'

The guard pushes the register towards him. 'Then you have to sign in.'

While he signs the register – John Jones from Microsoft is the best he can come up with – he feels the guard's eyes on him and, as he steps into the lift, he sees the guard pick up the phone. He gets out on the first floor and doubles backs down the fire escape stairs. He pushes the door slightly open and listens. 'Yes, that's right, a John Jones, been up to you a couple of times this week.' There is a pause and the guard continues, 'Nobody by that name? I'll be right up.' He waits until he hears the lift doors shutting, then quickly leaves the building. There'll be no coming back here. In any case, after his first sighting of Louise on the steps of Datagroup's offices, he has not managed to see her here again.

At night he has no better luck. Twice more he drives down from Highgate to Kentish Town. Once her apartment is lit, but he doesn't see her or her companion.

He sees little of his housemates. They have usually left for work when he returns from duty in the mornings; in the afternoons he leaves before they get back. When he does encounter one of them he detects an awkwardness that wasn't there before – clearly they have been discussing him.

Monica doesn't give up about the theatre. He caves in and swaps with Krzysztof, the Polish guard, which means that he'll have to work a double shift on Sunday.

On Friday evening he travels by tube to Kilburn. The journey from West Kensington seems interminable, and he feels tired and depressed. Monica is waiting for him on the steps of the Tricycle Theatre. She has had her hair cut and is wearing a thick coat and long scarf. He kisses her on the cheek; she smells of mint and perfume. 'You look very nice,' he says.

She smiles. 'Thank you.'

In the foyer a crowd is milling around. Everywhere people are eyeing each other and talking loudly. He walks over to the bar and orders two coffees. He feels out of place among these voluble people with their excited chatter. He and Monica go to a corner, light cigarettes.

A few minutes later a bell rings and they take their seats in the stalls. The interior of the theatre looks different from what he expected: smaller, more intimate. The stage, still dark, extends into the audience. The seats are narrow and close together and his knee presses against Monica's leg. He remembers high school: going to Sterland with Louise on a Friday night to see something like *Grease* or *Blue Lagoon*. And here he is, eighteen years later, on a date again. If only Louise could see him now.

The lights dim, a spotlight illuminates an armchair, gradually the rest of the stage lights up. It looks like a furniture warehouse of sorts: a jumble of wardrobes, chairs, tables, a large harp, bookcases, rolled-up carpets. A man dressed in a police uniform walks on, surveys the stage, touches a harp, walks around, then bursts out laughing. He is already bored; the gestures of the actor seem exaggerated, and it looks as if there's going to be little action. A woman comes in through a door; the policeman's wife, it transpires. And it's not a warehouse, as he initially thought, but the childhood home of Victor, the policeman.

He listens with half an ear to Victor and his wife arguing, while thinking of Louise. But then some words catch his attention. 'I look at my life and the whole thing is incomprehensible to me,' Victor is saying. 'I know all the reasons and all the reasons and all the reasons, and it ends up – nothing.'

He shifts in his seat, his attention now on what is happening on the stage. An old man wearing a yarmulke comes onto the stage: Solomon, a furniture trader. The furniture in the apartment is that of Victor's recently deceased father, which Solomon wants to buy. Victor and Solomon haggle; there's mention of Victor's wealthier older brother, Walter, and an argument ensues over the value of the furniture. Then Walter appears, smartly dressed and self-confident.

He glances at Monica's programme. The play is called *The Price*, not *The Prize*, as he thought he had heard Monica say earlier. And on stage there is a lot of haggling about the price of the furniture. Gradually he realises the play is really about other prices: how much Walter is willing to pay Victor to assuage his guilty conscience for leaving Victor to care for their ailing father while he went off to study, the price Victor had paid by staying with their father and sacrificing his own study plans.

Afterwards, on the pavement outside, he suggests that they go for a drink, it is only ten o'clock. They go into a pub down the road. The accents of the patrons are similar to Fergal Kennedy's; the mounted television is showing a replay of the recent Ireland–France Five Nations rugby international. Monica and he stand at the bar; he orders a pint of lager and a glass of white wine.

Monica asks, 'So, did you enjoy it?'

'I did, I did – but maybe it should have been called *The Choice*, don't you think? After all, it's all about making choices, isn't it?'

She nods, and sips from her glass. 'And you, Paul, how are you? You were not looking so good this week.'

He is in a strange and reckless mood; he wants to tell her about Louise. Why he doesn't know. Maybe because they are pressed against each other in the crowded bar.

'I'm fine. But I had a surprise this week … I bumped into someone I knew quite well in South Africa.'

She looks at him intently. 'A girl?'

'Yes.'

'She was your girlfriend in South Africa?'

'Something like that.'

'And you still like her?'

'I don't know.'

'Why did you break up?'

'Some things happened. It's difficult to explain.'

She puts her hand on his forearm. 'Is that why you come to London?'

But he has reached the end of his ability to confide. 'No, it was just a coincidence.'

'But you want her back, no?'

He shakes his head. 'No, no, that's all in the past.'

'You are confused?'

He manages to chuckle. 'No, not really, it was just a bit of a shock seeing her again.' Time to change the topic, he decides. 'And you, Monica, what about you – no boyfriends?'

She smiles. 'I had a friend in Prague, but I think he has someone else now. He wasn't happy that I come to London.'

A table frees up in a corner. He orders another round while Monica secures the seats. Everyone in the pub looks happy – Friday night euphoria. An uncomplicated life, he thinks: work, pub, an apartment or terraced house somewhere, football on the weekend. A society with resolvable problems.

When the pub closes he walks with her to the bus stop. Everywhere people are streaming out of restaurants and pubs. When the bus arrives he bends to kiss her on the cheek. But she turns her head so that he has to kiss her on the mouth, and then she hugs him.

He walks back to the tube station. Only in the carriage does he realise that he hasn't thought of Louise for several hours. As the train makes its way through the tunnels, he remembers something Victor said: 'It's that you've got to make decisions before you know what's involved, but you're stuck with the results anyway.' Yes, he thinks, with that he would agree.

Two weeks before the end of their basic training at Saldanha Bay Naval Base they were marched by their instructors to the parade ground and ordered to sit in the pavilion on the western border. The parade ground overlooked the sea, and the glare from the bay was blinding. Next to him sat two friends from school, Wouter and Anton, their uniforms stained with sweat patches. Above them in the cloudless and shimmering sky seagulls drifted lethargically on air currents. In front of the pavilion were officers and non-commissioned officers from different branches of the Navy and Army: Infantry, Marines, Diving, Communications, Transport and so on. The officers were there to recruit suitable candidates for their units, the training warrant officer bellowed. It was a welcome break from their daily routine of waking at four-thirty to get their barracks and kit ready for morning inspection, breakfast at six, physical training from seven to eleven, lectures until lunchtime, weapons training and drilling until late afternoon, then cleaning their rifles and the barracks and, finally, washing and ironing their kit until midnight.

The various representatives explained briefly what their units did, and what attributes potential candidates should have. The last speaker was a wiry officer of medium build wearing a purple beret, with paratrooper wings stitched above his left shirt pocket, and a badge – an inverted knife within a laurel wreath – above his right pocket. He introduced himself as Captain de Wet from 2 Reconnaissance Regiment. Whispers rippled through the pavilion. Who hadn't heard of the famous recces, the formidable Special Forces of the Defence Force?

They fell silent when the captain started talking. The Special Forces training, he said, was the most arduous – mentally and physically – in the Defence Force. It took a year to be trained as an operator, followed by another year of specialised training in the specific field of operations of whatever reconnaissance regiment they were posted to. But the end product, according to the captain, was a superb soldier – measured not only in terms of his military knowledge and skills but also by his capacity to endure mentally and physically. It was impossible, he warned them, to complete the initial two-month selection phase on physical resources alone – only those with tremendous psychological strength would make it. The pass rate in the selection phase was less than five per cent; in some years no one made it. Special Forces accepted only volunteers, and you could drop off the course at any time. But at the start of the course a prospective operator had to undertake – assuming he successfully completed the training – to sign up for an additional three years Permanent Force service after his initial two years National Service.

The captain's warning had sunk in, for when he asked for volunteers for the initial two-day physical testing phase not one of the thousand-odd National Servicemen in the pavilion stirred. He briefly considered volunteering, then decided against it. Not that he was scared of the physical challenge. He was as fit as he had ever been, and at school he had been a loose forward for first team. But five years in the army – that was too long. By the end of his Matric year he still did not know what career he wanted to pursue; he had vague ideas of studying, and then going into commerce of sorts. But he was weary of books and classrooms, and most of his friends were first going to do National Service. He had also looked forward to military service; friends' older brothers who had served on the border had returned with stirring tales of skirmishes with terrorists.

But then, volunteers started coming forward here and there. Without warning, Anton got up and walked down to the parade ground. He was surprised: Anton was smaller and weaker than him and hadn't exactly been the most enthusiastic trainee up to then. Wouter and he looked at each other. Wouter shook his head and then said, 'What the fuck,' and also stood up. He felt embarrassed. Two of his friends had just volunteered for the toughest branch of the Defence Force. How would it look back home if he did not? Not only Wouter and Anton but others too would think he had been too afraid to try, too afraid to put himself to the test. Without further thought, he stood up.

17

Early Saturday morning in Kentish Town. McDonald's is not yet open, so he sits in a bus shelter from where he can watch the house. The street is quiet; only occasionally does a vehicle speed past, splashing through pools of water.

Hours trickle past. People go in and out of the house, but of her there is no sign. Later he dials her number from the phone booth further down the street, but an answering machine picks up, a mechanical voice answering. It is unlikely that she would have left before he got here this morning, he thinks. She must have spent the night somewhere else; at the boyfriend's probably, but that doesn't bear thinking about.

It is still a few hours before he has to go on duty. He decides to walk to Regal's offices instead of going home. The walk will kill time and the exercise will do his knee good. After twenty minutes he reaches Hampstead Heath. The tepid February sun has lured people out of their houses. Muffled-up children run around, dogs bark, couples walk hand in hand. He leaves the gravelled path and walks across a field towards a hill where people are flying kites. He sits on a park bench and watches them. The kites look like postage stamps against the pale blue sky, and high above them a jetliner leaves a white scar in its wake. In the distance he can see the London Eye. A respectable-looking old man in a tweed jacket joins him on the bench. The man takes off his shoes and socks and stretches his legs out. None of the passers-by take any notice of him.

In this city you can do anything, even disappear, he thinks. Czechs, Poles, Chinese, Somalis, Iraqis, Pakistanis, Jamaicans – London accepts and absorbs all, including hundreds of thousands of his countrymen, many of them Afrikaners settling in the country that had a century earlier decimated their ancestors. And the English, the native English, did not seem to be too interested in the newcomers. They lived their own, private lives; they did not ask questions and, in turn, did not want to be questioned. That suited him fine.

And he could *really* disappear if he wanted to. At work he has struck up a relationship of sorts with Krzysztof, who had been a policeman in Poland but, according to him, earned a lot more in London than he ever did in Krakow. A week or so earlier he had mentioned to Krzysztof that his visitor's visa expired in a couple of months. That was no problem, said Krzysztof: he knew people who for a thousand pounds could get him a British passport. In fact, the passport would be issued by their contact at the Home Office.

But then again, what difference would a new identity make? A familiar dread comes over him, the knowledge that he has lost his way, that his life has derailed. Louise is a way back, a bridge to the past and the future.

At the end of Matric they had made no explicit promises to each other, but it was understood that she would wait for him. And when he was in the Army, he was able to visit her only a couple of times a year, but she wrote to him. And how he looked forward to those letters. When they returned to the base after an operation, there would sometimes be several letters for him. He would read and reread the letters, sniff them for a trace of her scent, analyse then for clues about her feelings for him. But her letters were matter-of-fact: university events, study results, holidays – normal student life. And she always ended her letters with bland statements of affection. She also mentioned that from time to time she bumped into André, who had become a leading figure in the anti-conscription movement at the University of Cape Town.

The man next to him pulls on his shoes and walks off. He is alone again. If he had to drop dead right now, he thinks, on a February afternoon, right here, on this hill in the south-east corner of this island, how would they know who he was? He carries nothing on him by which he could be identified, not even a credit card. And what would they make of Louise's wedding ring in his pocket? His housemates would realise after a day or two that he hadn't been home, or maybe when someone from Regal phoned. But they would probably assume that he had skedaddled, the few items of clothing and the sleeping bag he had left behind quid pro quo for his unpaid rent.

Two hours later he is busy changing into his uniform when Fergal Kennedy comes into the locker room.

'Paul, have you got a couple of minutes? I'd like to chat to you in my office.'

'Sure.' Has there been a complaint, he wonders, as he finishes dressing. Maybe a resident has noticed his absence during one of his nightly excursions to Kentish Town. It would be a pity if he is fired; the job is easy and he will miss Rex.

But Fergal smiles when he walks into his office a couple of minutes later. 'Sit down, sit down.' When he is seated Fergal leans forward on his elbows. 'So Paul, still happy here?'

'Yes, no complaints.'

'And how long are you planning to be with us?'

'I've got no fixed plans. But my visa expires in a couple of months.'

Fergal leans back in his swivel chair and folds his hands on his stomach. 'That can be fixed.'

'What do you mean?'

'I'll get to that. But first – I don't mean to pry, but given your background and academic qualifications, why are you working as a guard?'

He considers his answer, then decides it is better to give a sanitised version of the truth. 'It's a bit embarrassing. My fiancée left me and came over to London. I'm here to try and patch things up with her.'

Fergal rocks forward. 'Any success so far?'

'Not much, I'm afraid.'

'And if you do make up with her, what are your plans then? Will you be going back to South Africa?'

'I don't know, I suppose it depends on her.'

'Paul, I think you're wasting your time patrolling a street. I hear good things about you from the duty supervisors. And then there's that incident in Highgate, which I thought you handled well. I could definitely use someone like you better.'

He is surprised to feel flattered. 'Thank you.'

'I want to open a branch in Ealing later this year. A couple of vehicles at first, then growing the business as we get more clients. I need someone to run it for me, someone whom the guards and duty supervisors will respect but who can handle the office work. Obviously that person will have to be a permanent employee on a fixed salary, which will be substantially higher than that of a guard.' Fergal picks up a sheet of paper and reads aloud, 'Thirty-two thousand pounds a year, to be precise.' He looks up. 'Interested?'

First Captain Harris, now Fergal – seems that he has a hidden talent for security work. Thirty-two thousand pounds – a fortune compared to what he currently earns but a sum he would have considered a mediocre bonus when he was a bond trader at DAB Securities.

'What about my visa?' he asks.

'I'm sure we'll manage to arrange a work permit for you if you want to take things forward, and you're willing to commit for at least a year.'

He decides to play for time. 'Thank you very much. Can I think about it and get back to you?'

Fergal nods. 'Of course, of course, no rush. Think about it for a week or two, then we'll talk again.'

Monica visits earlier than usual. He gets out of the van and kisses her on the cheek.

'Thanks again for last night,' he says. 'I really enjoyed the play.'

She smiles. 'Do you want some coffee?'

'Sure, that's sounds good.'

'Come with me,' she says and turns back towards the house.

He hesitates. 'What about the Sturgeons?'

'I told you – they're away for the weekend.' She wags her finger at him. 'You don't listen.'

Monica unlocks the large front door. He follows her inside, through the marbled entrance hall, past a sweeping staircase and into an airy kitchen with copper pots and pans hanging from overhead wooden beams. She opens a stainless steel fridge and takes out a chocolate cake; inside he sees neatly arranged bottles of wine, pâtés and spreads, a bowl of strawberries. Monica switches on the percolator. They talk while they wait for the coffee to filter.

It is warm in the kitchen and Monica pulls off her jersey. Her T-shirt accentuates her breasts. He looks away quickly, but too late: she has noticed his glance.

He carries the tray with coffee and cake through to the living room. CNN is showing on a plasma screen hanging from the wall. He places the tray carefully on a low glass table. He has become used to more austere living and, in his uniform and boots, feels out of place in this large room with its thick carpet and large paintings and shelves of books. Monica picks up a remote control and mutes the television.

He sits down on a leather couch. When she leans forward to pour the coffee, the back of her shirt pulls up, exposing her lower back. A faint line of downy hair runs down her spine and into the cleft of her buttocks. He surprises himself by putting his hands on her hips and pulling her towards him. Their teeth scrape as they fall back on the leather couch. Her agile tongue snakes in his mouth. They undress quickly, silently; only when he struggles to pull off his boots does she giggle. Her breasts brush his chest, and her hair hangs over his face. When he feels that he is on the verge, he turns her around so that he is on top. His manoeuvre buys him a couple of minutes, but then he can hold back no longer and with a groan he gives way.

They lie intertwined, their bodies sticking together. Eventually she lifts herself on her elbow and looks down at him. 'You are very strange. I was thinking you don't like me in that way.'

'Well, obviously you were wrong,' he says, smiling.

She leans down and kisses him on the forehead. 'You are funny, I like that.'

Funny – that's a word that's not often been applied to him.

She leans down and kisses him on the forehead. 'And I like you too.'

'You don't want to get involved with me.' He pauses. How to say it? 'You don't know me, I'm bad news.'

She smiles. 'Relax, you too serious. I don't want to marry you, don't worry.'

The next morning he drives from Highgate to Park Royal to work Krzysztof's shift at a DHL depot. He thinks of Monica. Last night had been good, very good, but that's all it was or can be. But he has warned her, and maybe she was right, maybe he should just enjoy it for what it was, a friendship that seemed now to include sex. He feels a stab of desire at the memory of her under him, her legs clamped around his hips, her hair spread out on the leather couch.

As for Louise, wherever she's been for the weekend, she'll probably be back today. He is not on duty tonight; he will go back to Kentish Town this evening, he decides.

At a traffic light on the North Circular he glances at the van's side mirror. Behind him is a large white van. The man sitting on the passenger side seems familiar. He looks again to make sure. There can be no doubt: the shaven head, the nose-guard, the piggish eyes. And behind the steering wheel is the body-builder.

When he drives off his foot trembles on the accelerator. The van follows him. He decides not to reveal that he knows he is being followed.

He should have expected them to show up again, he realises. A few days after their first encounter a police officer had visited him at Regal's offices to take a formal statement. According to the officer they could charge the men only with possession of an illegal weapon: they had not harmed Monica, and she had not seen Adam Stubbs trying to stab him;

it was his word against theirs. Both men had extensive police records: possession of drugs, drunk and disorderly conduct, assault (committed by the body-builder, a nightclub bouncer named Carl Makewell, for which had served six months), dealing in stolen goods. Very dodgy characters, the officer informed him. But, he added with a slight smile, Mr Stubbs would need some orthopaedic work and Mr Makewell was in hospital with concussion.

The van follows him all the way to the warehouse, taking care to stay a couple of cars behind him. When he turns into DHL's yard it speeds past. He relieves the night guard, makes himself a cup of coffee in the booth at the entrance. While he eats the sandwich Monica had brought him just before he left that morning he keeps an eye on the street, but there is no sign of the van or the men. There is little risk of being attacked here: the depot is closed on a Sunday and the gate is locked.

They are bent on revenge, that much is clear. They are probably trying to find out where he lives, as they already know where he works. He considers their likely strategy. While he on duty he is a difficult target as he will more than likely be on the alert. Their chances are much better when he is off duty, or at home. But now they have lost one of their biggest advantages, the element of surprise. He considers his alternatives. He could contact the police, but what would that achieve? He can't prove that they were following him, and even if he could, what could the police do? He will have to take care of it himself, he decides.

He wonders at the rush of excitement he feels. This is something he can handle. And it has been a long time since that has been the case. He will choose the time and place of their next encounter.

MR MAUBANE: Mr du Toit, is it not so that you considered yourself to be part of an elite unit, a cut above the rest of the Defence Force?

MR DU TOIT: I would not say that. We were better trained, that is true.

MR MAUBANE: Mr du Toit, how were you wounded? What were the circumstances?

MR DU TOIT: It was during a military operation in Angola.

MR MAUBANE: What kind of military operation? Please be so kind as to give us more details.

MR DU TOIT: How is that relevant?

MR MAUBANE: Mr du Toit, I ask the questions, if you don't mind.

MR VAN VUUREN: Mr Chairman, I'm sure I don't have to remind my learned colleague that this committee has no jurisdiction over incidents that took place outside the borders of South Africa.

MR MAUBANE: Chairperson, I want to get some insight into the background of the applicant, his character, the things he was involved in.

CHAIRPERSON: Mr Maubane, it is up to the witness whether he wants to answer you or not.

MR MAUBANE: Mr du Toit?

MR DU TOIT: I don't think any of that is relevant here.

MR MAUBANE: So you will not answer my question?

MR DU TOIT: That is correct.

MR MAUBANE: I see. If I may ask, how do you feel today about your service in the Special Forces?

MR DU TOIT: I feel proud. We had outstanding successes in the field. Black and white, we fought side by side, we were a totally non-racial unit.

MR MAUBANE: And how many of these black people were South Africans?

MR DU TOIT: A few. I cannot recall.

MR MAUBANE: Is it not so that the majority, if not all, of your Black members were Angolan rebels, or the like, who had joined the South African Defence Force after they had been defeated by the legitimate Angolan government?

MR DU TOIT: There were some.

MR MAUBANE: So you are proud of the fact that you fought with mercenaries in an illegal war in Angola?

MR DU TOIT: I was serving my country. I know there was a Communist threat, despite what is said today. We were professional soldiers. The decisions were made by the politicians.

MR MAUBANE: Were you also proud that you made war on un-armed civilians when you left the formal Defence Force structures? This morning in your statement you made much about the proud history of the Afrikaners. Do you think

General de Wet or any of those Boer War generals would have waged war against unarmed civilians?

MR DU TOIT: Those were different times, different people. I don't think you can compare. As I explained, the ANC had brought the war into the country, they were the ones who were using civilians. We had to counter that threat. But today I think that the Defence Force should not have been involved in internal security, it should have been left to the police. That is why I eventually resigned.

MR MAUBANE: So you agree that you knew what you were doing was wrong, even then?

MR DU TOIT: I thought it was wrong that the Defence Force was involved. I did not think it was wrong that we fought the enemy.

MR MAUBANE: These operations you took part in while you were a student at UCT, did you think it was lawful to plant bombs, vandalise cars and so on?

MR DU TOIT: I was told I would be indemnified should we ever be implicated.

MR MAUBANE: Please answer my question. Do you agree that you knew you were taking part in illegal activities?

MR DU TOIT: I was told that the Defence Force and therefore the State had approved the projects, and that we would not be prosecuted should we be caught because the country was facing a total onslaught, and that we were effectively in a state of war with Communism. The projects were aimed at enemies of the Republic of South Africa, against whom the South African Police could not act.

MR MAUBANE: But you knew these so-called projects were illegal?

MR DU TOIT: Under normal circumstances I would agree with you. But the circumstances were not normal.

MR MAUBANE: Mr du Toit, you were engaged in criminal activities.

MR DU TOIT: I know what is a crime and what is not a crime. I was following lawful instructions, within the context of the times and the context of what we were doing.

MR MAUBANE: I don't understand. How is it possible to give a lawful instruction to commit a crime?

MR DU TOIT: I agree that it may not be technically possible to do so, but my acceptance of the instructions was not made on a legal technical basis, it was made in the context of us being at war.

MR MAUBANE: Mr du Toit, you have a strange way with words. In your language a project means the killing of people, and the word lawful has to be interpreted in the context of the times. I put it to you that lawful has an unchangeable legal technical meaning, and that there's no other way of understanding what is lawful other than by looking at the law?

MR DU TOIT: Words mean what people decide they mean.

MR MAUBANE: Only in Alice in Wonderland, Mr du Toit. Nevertheless, I don't want to engage in a philosophical debate. Why did you obey these commands?

MR DU TOIT: I think it was a matter of obedience. Of course I know today that what I did back then was wrong. But I mean, how can I sit here today and tell you thirteen years later in a totally different South Africa why I thought back then it was lawful other than by saying to you that I had an instruction and I felt that that instruction had to be executed within the set-up that I was employed in.

MR MAUBANE: If Captain Harris had ordered you to murder a civilian, would you have obeyed his order?

MR DU TOIT: Of course not.

MR MAUBANE: But you did obey his order to plant a limpet mine in a hall used by civilians, a situation in which it could have been reasonably envisaged that civilians would be killed, were in fact killed as it turned out?

MR DU TOIT: As I said earlier, the intention was not to harm anyone. And the project was aimed at the ECC, which was a well-known enemy of the State.

MR MAUBANE: In what way?

MR DU TOIT: They opposed the Defence Force. They advised people not to report for military duty and that was a thorn in the flesh of the Defence Force.

MR MAUBANE: Did they commit any acts of violence?

MR DU TOIT: Not that I'm aware of.

MR MAUBANE: But you considered them to be enemies of the State?

MR DU TOIT: Yes.

MR MAUBANE: So in your reckoning any member of the ECC, or for that matter any anti-apartheid organisation, was a potential enemy of the State?

MR DU TOIT: In a way, yes.

MR MAUBANE: Mr du Toit, do you have any idea how many members the ECC had, or the collective anti-apartheid movement?

MR DU TOIT: I can't say. Hundreds of thousands, maybe?

MR MAUBANE: And all of these people were enemies of the State, against whom covert action would be justified?

MR DU TOIT: Not necessarily. It would depend on their exact actions.

MR MAUBANE: And who would make this determination?

MR DU TOIT: The intelligence structures, MI, National Intelligence, bodies like that.

MR MAUBANE: So if Captain Harris came to you and said, 'Military Intelligence has determined that Mr X is a threat to the State, and I want you to kill him', would you have obeyed?

MR DU TOIT: No, I would not have murdered civilians.

MR MAUBANE: But why then not? You've told us that it was war, and that you were a soldier who obeyed instructions, and in war soldiers are expected to kill, are they not?

MR DU TOIT: That is so. But I would not have taken part in a project whose objective was the killing of civilians.

MR MAUBANE: Mr du Toit, I put it to you that you are talking nonsense. It is common knowledge that in those years the Defence Force, especially the Special Forces units, undertook operations in neighbouring countries in which civilians were killed.

MR DU TOIT: Those deaths were unfortunate but accidental. In any war civilians sometimes get caught in the crossfire, for example Hiroshima, Vietnam, there are many examples.

MR MAUBANE: Are you not forgetting one crucial distinction here? A country's military is there to be deployed against other countries' military forces, not against the citizens of its own country. I put it to you that you knew you were engaged in illegal activities, and you had the choice of not obeying orders, but that in fact you volunteered to take part in criminal activities.

MR DU TOIT: Is that a question? I have already given my position on that.

MR MAUBANE: Let me be more specific. You present yourself as a loyal soldier who was just obeying orders. But you say you would not have obeyed an order to kill a civilian. But then you were not a blind automaton, you had discretion. You could therefore apply your judgement as to what was a lawful order, and what was not. Now Captain Harris comes along and says, Go and plant a limpet bomb in a hall used by civilians. What would have happened if you had refused to obey that order? Could you have been court-martialled?

MR DU TOIT: I don't know.

MR MAUBANE: Oh, come now, Mr du Toit. You know that you could not have been court-martialled. A soldier can only be court-martialled for disobeying lawful orders. You were part of a secret unit, acting outside of the law. So you knew all along that you were engaged in illegal activities, and that you didn't have to obey unlawful commands. You willingly participated in criminal activities. Since when does a soldier have to be guaranteed indemnity when he goes off to war? It is accepted in international law that soldiers cannot be prosecuted for obeying lawful orders in lawful wars. But your situation was different, wasn't it?

MR DU TOIT: I have explained my situation.

18

This time he is in luck: her apartment lights are on. He again watches from the phone booth. He sees figures moving behind her curtains, but he cannot identify them. Once more he reads the cards of the prostitutes pasted against the side of the booth; by now he knows their faces and names by heart. Later a fog descends, a grey sheet that shrouds the street and dims the streetlights. And suddenly he has had enough, enough of hiding. He knows everything he needs to know.

He leaves the booth and walks towards the house. He is still about twenty yards away from the front door when it opens and a man comes out onto the steps. It is the boyfriend, he sees when he gets closer. He considers turning around and walking away; it is not yet too late, he has not been seen. Then Louise comes out. She glances at him but turns back to the man. He has the hood of his anorak over his head; she has obviously not recognised him. His left hand trembles when he pushes open the gate. Now they both look at him. Her face is thinner than before. He pulls down his hood and watches her face. After a second or two he sees her eyes widen.

'Hallo, Louise.'

She looks at him silently.

'How are you?' he says. His voice sounds strained.

'Paul,' she whispers.

Louise's friend looks at him with cautious interest – or is it apprehension he detects?

He thrusts his hand out. 'Hallo.'

The man takes his hand tentatively. 'Adrian.' His mouth is soft, his hair gelled.

Nobody speaks. A car with a faulty muffler roars down the street.

She breaks the silence. 'What are you doing here?'

'You know.'

Adrian, who obviously doesn't understand Afrikaans, gives her a concerned look. 'Everything okay, Louise?' He pronounces her name as Liwheeze, he notes with irritation. But he must do nothing to aggravate the situation.

'How did you find me?' Her voice is louder than before.

'Can we talk?'

She folds her arms across her chest and examines him.

'In private,' he adds.

She turns to Adrian. 'I'll phone you tomorrow, okay?'

Adrian takes her hand. 'Are you sure?'

She nods.

Adrian walks away, but after a dozen or so yards he stops and turns around. When Louise gives him a small wave he walks on.

'I suppose you want to come in?'

'Please.'

He is short of breath as he follows her into an entrance hall with a chequerboard floor and a large gilt-framed mirror on the wall. But patches of peeling paint disfigure the wall around the mirror and there are dark stains on the carpeting of the stairs. They walk up two flights of stairs, past the closed doors of the other apartments. She does not look back to see whether he is following her. They go into her flat. On a wooden coffee table in the lounge he sees an empty wine bottle and two glasses. The room looks well settled: rows of books on two shelves, a comfortable sofa and armchair, a computer and printer on a desk against the wall.

Louise sits down in the arm chair. He stays on his feet.

'Who's your friend?' he asks, his voice hoarse. Not a good start.

She frowns. 'Please sit down.'

But he can't stop himself. 'How long?'

He sees her hands gripping the armrests. 'Paul, what are you doing here?'

'Are you serious?'

She shakes her head. 'I heard you'd disappeared – I should have guessed. How did you find me?' She gives a forced laugh. 'Oh, how could I forget? You were a spy, weren't you?' There are two red spots high on her cheeks. She is more desirable than ever.

He sits down on the sofa. 'Please, Louise. I didn't come here to fight.'

She crosses her legs. 'What do you want?'

'You're still my wife, are you not? I think you at least owe me an explanation.' It feels as though he's talking to a stranger who happens to have Louise's body and face.

She leans forward. 'An explanation! After what came out at the hearing!'

'But you heard my reasons, my answers.'

'You mean that wonderful tale about the Voortrekkers and the Boer War, and how you wanted to fight Communism and how it was all for your country and the volk – yes, I heard all that.'

'That was true.'

She laughs harshly. 'Come off it. Leave that for the judges and lawyers. Since when had you been interested in all that?'

'Just because I didn't talk about those things doesn't mean I didn't believe in them.'

'There are many things you didn't talk about, it seems. But I'm not going to sit here and argue with you.' She shifts in the armchair as though preparing to stand up. 'What do you want from me?'

'We never talked again about what happened, about André, about you and me. You just disappeared. I can't do that. I need to understand.'

She shrugs. 'What's there to understand? You killed André, you lied to me, I left you.'

'When did I lie? I told you everything before the hearing, so why did you not leave then?'

Her eyes glitter. 'You told me everything, sure. But what about the two white men in the car near the hall just before the bomb exploded? You didn't tell me about that, did you? And we both know that you knew that André was in the ECC long before you went to UCT. So why then did you testify that you only found out when you were at UCT? And I remember wondering at the time why you went to UCT rather than Stellenbosch. Oh yes, now I remember: you thought UCT had a better commerce faculty.' She snorts. 'And you still want me to believe that it was an accident.'

His answers are ready, he has rehearsed them many times. 'I went to UCT because the Defence Force was paying. It was either that or staying in the Army. I still had a year left on my PF contract, remember? And it also meant that I didn't have to go to my father for money to go to university. As for the car: I wasn't there or in that car, so how could I tell you about it? And yes, I did know about André being in the ECC. But I didn't want to admit it, because the TRC would have wanted to find out how I knew, and you would have been dragged into it.'

'So you lied to protect me, is that it?' She looks at him. 'Paul, where were you that night?'

'As I said, in my room in Rondebosch.'

'I tried to call you a few times that evening. There was no answer.'

His face feels hot. So this is her trump card, the coup de grâce. 'You're wrong – I was there. Maybe I had gone out to the shop when you phoned, I don't remember. And how can you be sure after all this time that you phoned that evening?'

'I remembered when the advocate asked you where you were that night. You were coming to me the next day for the weekend, remember? But I phoned you that night to tell you that I had to finish coding a program, and that the only slot I could get on the university mainframe was on the Friday evening. But I couldn't get hold of you, and the next day you waited for me the whole evening at my flat. That's when you told me André was dead, remember?' She dabs at her eyes and gets up. 'Please go. Now.'

He remains seated. 'Do you really believe I wanted him dead? Why would I have wanted that?' He has asked the question, it is out in the open, he has called check.

She turns around. The question hangs in the air. For a few seconds they look at each other. Then she sighs. 'Paul, it's over. Sign the papers,' she says, and walks to the door.

He remembers their frenetic love-making on their last night together. 'But that night, that night before the hearing, why that?' He sees the back of her neck redden, but she doesn't turn around or answer him. A dull ache has spread from his chest to his limbs. He gets up. At the door he asks. 'Can I see you again?'

She shakes her head and opens the door.

He takes out a pen and his tube ticket. 'Let me at least leave my telephone number.'

She looks on silently as he writes on the back of the ticket.

19

Large, wet snowflakes are drifting down like confetti on the cars and pedestrians when he comes out of Baron's Court station. The gates of the cemetery are locked. He pulls himself up the wall, drops into the graveyard. He slips as he hits the ground, under his palms he feels the soggy earth. He struggles to find the path in the dark. It is quiet, as if the falling snow absorbs every sound. All he hears is his own breathing, and on his face he feels the light touch of falling snow.

He feels his way forward gingerly. He is alone in the cemetery and feels calmer than when he left Louise's apartment an hour earlier. And to his surprise he feels rested, despite having slept only an hour or two in the last two days. It is as if the night envelops him, embraces him. Underfoot surely lie thousands, their bones crumbling in rotting caskets. Who remembers them, their problems, their lives?

When he lets himself into the house, he is greeted by its distinctive odour, an unpleasant compound of damp carpets, dust and cigarette smoke. He pauses at the entrance to the lounge, chats briefly to Steve and Marius who are watching television. Then he goes up to his room and lies down on the bed. The room is cold and the vapour of his breath and the cigarette smoke fog up the air.

His earlier mood lingers. She had seemed like a stranger. How could you have lived for someone for so long, have known them for even longer, and yet feel that way? What he had feared had come to pass: she thought that he had intended to kill André. Even worse, that he had actually killed André.

And the truth? The truth had somehow slipped away, not only from him but also from the TRC. Between him and the truth was a curtain, and the shadows behind the curtain kept on moving and changing shape. And he could not bear to look at the curtain for too long. But all that mattered now was that she believed he had planned to kill André, and that he would have to convince her otherwise.

Then something occurs to him, a question that he should have asked her: if she had left because of what she had heard and remembered at the hearing, why had she already quit her job a week earlier?

What now? It seems that there are only two alternatives. He can give up and go home. But where is home? He has sold his car, his furniture is in storage, the house has been re-let, his savings are nearly depleted. As a bond dealer he will not work again, that much is clear. Of course, there's Captain Harris and his job offer. Full circle after fourteen years, Harris and he working side by side. Security work – is that all he is suited for now? That leaves his father and the farm. But that he will not do, never.

Or he could stay in London, chisel away at Louise, try to dislodge Adrian. It has been only four months, surely not enough time for her new life to have set. That's all he can really do, he realises. He will give her time to get used to the idea of his being in London. She hadn't even asked where he lived, or for how long he has been over here. Surely when the shock of seeing him wears off she will be curious? But until then he will have to stay away; now that she knows that he is here she will be on her guard.

Midweek he travels up to Hampstead to meet Monica. She does not work on Wednesday afternoons; they are going to see a film. He accepted her invitation readily, a welcome break in the daily grind of work and sleep and waiting for Louise to call. Outside Hampstead station he looks around to get his bearings. It is a blustery and overcast day, but the snow of three days earlier has melted. The streets are congested in all directions. Then he sees the cinema's sign across the road.

Monica waits in the small dark foyer, dressed in a ski anorak and jeans. Her hair is tied back, and her face glows. She kisses him on the mouth and they embrace briefly.

Their seats are on the balcony, a leather sofa on which they sit side by side. There is no one else on the balcony, and in the stalls below only a half-dozen solitary cinema-goers.

'Do you like where we sit?' Monica asks, taking his hand. 'It is special seats.'

Her hand is cold in his, her slender fingers as fragile as the bones of a small bird. 'Very nice. How much do I owe you?'

'My treat, okay?'

'Come on, Monica, I probably earn more than you.'

She squeezes his hand. 'Are you accountant or what? You can buy me a drink later.' She giggles. 'Maybe make me drunk, take advantage, okay?'

The lights dim. The movie – *Memento* – was her choice. He is engrossed from the start. The main character, Leonard, is looking for the man who raped and killed his wife. But in the same attack Leonard's short-term memory was damaged, so that although he can remember events from long ago, recent memories are immediately erased.

He has the same – but opposite – affliction as Leonard, he thinks. It was only after his marriage that that he gradually realised how much of his life he had forgotten. Louise could recollect vividly events and people from when she was two or three years old; his earliest memory is of a fall from a swing when he was seven. And sometimes a stranger would greet him in a in a restaurant or shopping centre and, to his embarrassment, it would transpire that they had been at school or university together, or had met in the course of his work. Sometimes their faces would be vaguely familiar, but the other details would stay tantalisingly out of reach. Or Louise would remind him of a party they had been to, or a film they had seen, and he would not be able to remember anything. Large swathes of his life were missing. From someone he had heard that everything you experienced was etched in your memory, that it was all still there, waiting to be retrieved. But it seems to him that most things just flickered through his consciousness without leaving a trace of their passing. And even when he does remember something, he is unsure to what extent the memory overlaps the actual event. You are a witness to your own life, but eyewitnesses are notoriously unreliable.

An hour into the film Monica leans her head on his shoulder and puts her hand on his thigh. She whispers in his ear. 'No one can see us, you know.'

He is immediately aroused. 'Monica, you are very naughty. I want to watch the film.'

She slides her hand over his groin and feels, then smiles. 'I don't think so.' She leans across and kisses him, while her hand fiddles with his zip. She twists, turns, pulls her jeans down to her ankles, then lowers herself on to him, her back to him, her feet on the floor, her hands on the balcony railing. At first she moves slowly, then faster, rhythmically thudding against him. He grips her tightly when he can hold back no longer; at the same time she gives a stifled cry. In the stalls below a cinema-goer shifts in his seat.

Monica falls back on her seat. She sighs and pulls up her denims, then kisses his ear. 'You are not bad for old man. I must go to toilet, you come a lot.' Her casual reference to his ejaculation is slightly disconcerting. But it's the best sex he's had for many years, he thinks as he waits for her to return. This is something other than he is used to, something more uncontrolled and wild and exciting.

Afterwards they walk down Hampstead High Street and she takes his hand. At first he feels awkward, but after a while he relaxes. It looks like an affluent area, judging from the many coffee shops, boutiques and restaurants. It is only a few minutes after four, but the shining headlights of the cars toiling up Rosslyn Hill are strung out into the distance.

This is not real life, he thinks, Monica can be no more than a pleasant interlude, a stop-gap. But he feels good, better than he has in months. He should feel guilty: he is using her to fill the cavity where Louise used to be, where Louise will again be. But he doesn't, and for the first time London seems bearable, more than bearable. In this city you could blend into the anonymous millions and make a fresh start, lead an uneventful life under the radar.

They go into a pub with large mirrors and a dozen or so drinkers sitting at the bar counter and small round tables. They order, then take their drinks to a counter at the street windows.

They clink their glasses and Monica says, winking, 'I think we must go to movies every day?'

'Monica, you are a bad girl, very bad.'

She laughs, throws back her head. 'But I think you like, no?'

He shakes his head in mock disapproval. A shaven-headed man walks past the window and he suddenly remembers the other morning. 'I've been meaning to ask you. Have you ever seen those men again, the men who were following you?'

She frowns. 'No, of course not. I will tell you. Why you ask?'

He shrugs. 'They were following me on Sunday morning.'

'You are sure?'

He nods. 'Yes, one hundred per cent.'

'But you must go to the police. They are bad people.'

'And tell the police what?' He sips from his pint. 'I've got no proof. But it's you I'm worried about. You must be careful, and you mustn't walk alone at night. When I'm on duty I can take you to the tube station, or fetch you.'

She nods her head. 'Sure, okay. But you, what you going to do?'

'I will sort it out.'

She puts her hand on his. 'The other night you tell me that I don't know you. Tell me something, where you learn to fight like that?'

'In the army. I was in the army for five years.' But that is not true, he thinks. The fighting had started much earlier, when he was fourteen or fifteen. He had fought during school breaks, at parties, at drive-ins, in parks. There had always been the opportunity, and he and his friends had never shied away. Early on he had learnt how to control his own fear, found out that the keys to victory were surprise and decisiveness, that you had to strike first, and strike hard, a headbutt or punch while your opponent was still getting ready.

'And what was your job in army?' Her eyes fix on him.

'I found out where enemy camps were, things like that.'

'But who was your enemy, the ANC?'

He is surprised: he had assumed that, as with most foreigners he met over here, she knew little of South Africa other than Mandela and apartheid. 'Yes, sometimes.'

'Who else?'

'SWAPO, the South West African People's Organisation, who wanted to take over what is now Namibia.'

'But you are South African. Why did you fight over Namibia?'

'I don't really remember.' And that is true, he realises. Reasons had been provided to him, that much he remembers, but he had not questioned those reasons; others had decided for him, and he had accepted that.

'And did you do bad things?'

'Yes.'

'Why?'

He looks out the window, then answers. 'It was war, I believed it was necessary.'

'Paul, we all make mistakes. But we do not have to make the same mistakes again. We can change; it is our decision.'

She squeezes his hand. Can you? he wonders. This belief some people have in transformation, a belief contrary to all the evidence – where does it come from? Were the grooves not imprinted at the beginning, and all that remained was for the record to play out?

20

Monday morning, a sky the colour of wet cement. He walks home through the cemetery, later than usual; there were long delays on the Piccadilly Line owing to signal failures. A week has passed since his meeting with Louise. She has not phoned, nor has he again ventured out to Kentish Town. He has been in London for three months, longer than he had foreseen at the outset, he thinks. Strange how quickly one falls into a different life, the daily journey to and from Regal's offices in Wembley now as familiar as his Johannesburg commute used to be.

It is only when the three men are ten yards away that he realises something is wrong. Twenty or so seconds before he had vaguely noted them walking towards him, and from their attire – jeans, muddied boots, canvas tool bags – he had assumed they were construction workers like Chris and JB.

But now they have stopped, and one has put his canvas bag on the path next to his feet. From the way they watch him it is clear that they are waiting for him. He stops. They regard him impassively. One of the men is tall, with a pitted face and puffy eyes; the other two – shorter, stockier – look like brothers. Then he hears footsteps rapidly approaching from behind. He swivels around. It is the body-builder, bearing down on him with a two-foot length of pipe. Close behind is his shaven-headed friend.

He is more angry than afraid. He was forewarned, he should have been more alert; it is his own fault. Two drunks he could manage, but not five prepared attackers – the only alternative is to flee. He feints a step to the left, then breaks to the right. But one of the brothers is fast, very fast, and blocks his intended escape route between two gravestones. On his right he sees the bodybuilder closing in, on his left the other three men. He drops his shoulder, charges straight ahead, hits the brother in the chest. They go down together, the man clutching at his anorak. He head butts him as they hit the ground, pulls loose, tries to get up. Then he feels a tremendous blow against his skull, as if he has been struck by a large rock. He falls on his side, against his cheek he feels grass and gravel. He tries to get up, but his limbs refuse to cooperate and he manages only to turn his head skywards. A moment passes, two, maybe he blanks out, for next the shaven-headed man is looming over him, the knife a cold smear of grey against the dark sky. Someone behind him says, 'For fuck's sake, Adam, finish him off so we can get the fuck out of here.'

So this is how it ends, he thinks. Not in fear but in resignation, not in his country but in this city of stone.

He wakes in a sunlit room. Across the room are two tidily made beds; in the bed next to him a sleeping old man hooked up to a drip. A hospital. He has survived it seems, but his head throbs, and his tongue is swollen. When he tries to move pain shoots through his side. He fingers his bandaged torso: broken ribs perhaps. What else? The top of his head is also bandaged, and his lower lip has stitches in it. But his arms and legs seem fine, his nose and teeth are intact. Why is he still alive?

A black nurse comes into the ward, pushing a metal trolley in front of her, 'Aha, you're awake now, you sleep too much,' she says.

Her accent is familiar. He reads her name tag – Ruth Dlamini. He is confused: has he somehow been transported to South Africa? 'Dumela, sisi,' he says. His tongue is heavy and he struggles to form the words. 'Where am I?'

She smiles broadly, lifts her hands. 'Goeiemore. I thought when I saw the name on the chart – that's a boertjie. You are in the Charing Cross Hospital. You came in this morning.' Her Afrikaans is near flawless.

He recalls walking past the bland concrete structure a couple of times; he is a kilometre or so from his lodgings. At the time he had wondered why the hospital had the same name as a West End street. 'What is wrong with me?'

She walks to the foot of his bed, reads his card. 'Four cracked ribs, possible concussion. You must rest. The doctor he will come now.'

'Please, sisi, some water?'

She shakes her head emphatically. 'Aikôna. You must not take anything until the doctor has seen you,' she says, pushing the trolley out of the ward. He looks at the clock over the door of the ward. It is half-past ten in the morning; he has been unconscious for three, maybe three and a half hours.

A hospital clerk with a stack of forms makes an appearance. He supplies his real name, but changes his address from 303 to 33 Whippet Road. He has no travel insurance, and does not want to be saddled with a bill; if caught out, he can always blame it on a clerical error.

The doctor, a pale and freckled youngster who looks about the same age as his housemates, comes by a few minutes later. The doctor asks him some questions, prods and pushes various parts of his body, tests his reflexes. He is lucky, he says; his injuries aren't serious. But because of the head injury he'll have to stay in the hospital for a couple of days for observation. What happened after the assault, or who brought him to the hospital, the doctor does not know. The police will be by later to take a statement.

He hobbles to a payphone in the corridor and phones the duty supervisor at Regal. He also leaves a message on the answering machine at the house.

At noon Nurse Dlamini returns with a trolley stacked with lunches. He questions her while she props up the pillows behind his back. She is from Durban, one of a dozen or so South African nurses who work at the hospital. In two months here she earns more than her annual salary at home but she is homesick for mieliepap and braaivleis, she tells him. She bustles efficiently around the ward and answers his questions briskly, but always with a smile.

After lunch the ward is quiet. His elderly ward companion is awake but has not yet spoken. From time to time a nurse walks past the entrance; later a cleaning team comes in to polish the floor. The familiar routines of hospital life, he remembers.

He had been unlucky, very unlucky. Their twelve-man team had outfitted themselves in enemy kit before they were choppered to the foothills of the Serra Techamalinde, rugged and mountainous territory in southern Angola. Their mission was to find and destroy a base camp used by SWAPO to infiltrate fighters across the Kunene River into South-West Africa. After the drop-off they had walked through the night. In the morning they found fresh tyre tracks. They established their observation post and hid on high ground, posted look-outs, then rested. Two hours later a Soviet Gaz truck approached from the south. That night they followed the tracks for thirty kilometres to the outskirts of an enemy base that was well hidden in a narrow valley with good ground and tree cover. The grass huts were spread out in an area about two hundred metres long and eighty metres wide and the only escape routes were to the north and south of the valley. A death trap.

They watched the base for the entire day and pinpointed the positions of the machine-guns and mortars and guards. As far as they could establish there were about seventy fighters in the base. After dark they planted the Claymore mines and set trip wires on both sides of the valley.

Two teams were deployed behind the mines while another team took up position with 81-mm mortars on the western side of the valley.

Sunrise was going to be at 05h40. But the two gunships arrived five minutes earlier, on schedule, the sound of their approach muffled by the surrounding hills. Surprise was total. There was a sudden roar of engines, then a cacophony as the mortars and the gunships' 20-mm cannons simultaneously opened fire. He was in the southern team. It was not long before they heard the first Claymores detonating. Not one fighter made it through their booby traps. The mortar and gunship assault lasted fifteen minutes.

When the Alouettes turned south and flew away they moved in. The ordance and ball ammunition had ripped through the grass huts and most were on fire. Suddenly an enemy fighter called out to them from the side, obviously fooled by their uniforms and black face paint. Captain Fourie cut him down with a short burst. Everywhere there were dead and dying, inside a burning hut a wounded man was screaming. They systematically swept the base, machine-gunning everything and everybody, including the wounded.

A few minutes later they were finished; the entire operation had lasted twenty-eight minutes. To the east the sky had turned dove grey, but a dark pall of smoke hung over the valley. He was lighting a cigarette when he felt a hammer blow to his knee; only then did he hear the crack of an AK-47.

Later, in 2 Military Hospital, he heard that the wounded fighter had concealed himself in thick undergrowth, the reason why they had not seen him during their sweep. The fighter had been shot in the right shoulder but had somehow managed to wedge his rifle against his left shoulder and pull the trigger.

He must have dozed off, for when he opens his eyes Nurse Dlamini is standing at the side of his bed, flanked by two uniformed police officers, a young woman and an older man. The man nods to Nurse Dlamini, who turns and leaves the ward.

'It is your lucky day, Mr du Toit,' the male detective says after introducing himself. 'Fortunately for you, two off-duty officers were walking through the cemetery when you were attacked. Your attackers fled when our officers made their presence known. I suspect your injuries would have been much worse if not for them.'

He sits down in the chair next to the bed, but the female officer remains standing, a notebook in her hand. The male detective opens a paper file. 'Any idea what gave rise to the attack, Mr du Toit, or who your attackers were?'

'No idea. Never seen them before. I was just walking home.'

The detective glances at his colleague, then looks at him. 'Are you sure?'

'Yes.'

The detective frowns. 'Where are you from?'

'South Africa.'

'And the purpose of your visit to London is?'

'Holiday.'

'According to our officers you were dressed in uniform.' He looks at the file. 'A security firm, I see. Presumably you have permission to work in this country?'

'Oh, it's just casual work, nothing permanent.'

'Some of our colleagues from the Home Office may want to meet with you. Your address please.'

He gives them the same address that he provided the hospital clerk. The female officer scribbles in her notebook. 'We will probably want to talk to you again,' the male detective says. He stands up and takes a card out of his wallet. 'If you happen to remember anything else.'

Afterwards he considers the events of the morning. The attack had been well planned: they knew his route, what time he came off duty, and they had ambushed him in the middle of the cemetery, the furthest point from the entrances. His head injury must have been inflicted by the body-builder's pipe, the cracked ribs from a kick or two.

Suddenly anger surges through him, so powerful that he has to grip the railings around the bed to still the shaking that takes hold of him. They had meant to kill him. They have escalated it, not him. And Monica is also probably in danger from these urban beasts of prey. There is only one way to end this.

Early evening he hears familiar voices approaching in the corridor. JB, Chris and Steve walk into the ward. He lifts his hand by way of greeting.

JB laughs nervously. 'Fucking hell, I hope the other guy looks worse.'

He shakes his head. 'Unfortunately not.'

'What the fuck happened?' Steve asks.

They cluster around his bed as he tells them; he does not disclose that he knows his assailants. Chris is indignant: after he is discharged from hospital they must seek vengeance; they are sure to find his attackers on the nearby council estate. JB and Steve agree – it is unacceptable that they should go unpunished.

He is unexpectedly moved by their show of support. They owe him nothing, and they seem sincere.

Steve says, 'Before I forget – a girl phoned for you.'

'Monica?'

'No, no, Louise. Sounded Afrikaans.'

'What did she want?'

'Just wanted to talk to you. I told her you were here.'

Then he sees Monica appear in the doorway, a shopping bag in one hand. She pushes past his housemates and takes his hand. 'The new guard says you were attacked.'

'I'm okay, nothing serious.' His three housemates are watching them with keen interest. 'Let me introduce you.'

His housemates are unusually abashed as she shakes their hands in turn. They shuffle round and make small talk for another few minutes, then excuse themselves and leave.

Monica looks at him. 'Who did this?'

'Same guys. This time they invited a few friends.'

She tightens her grip on his hand. 'No. Is my fault you get hurt.'

'No, no. I should have been more careful.'

'But now the police can lock them up?'

'I didn't tell the police. What's the point?'

'But what are you going to do?'

'I will finish it, don't worry.'

She shakes her head 'No, Paul. This is not the way.'

'Maybe.'

'Please.'

'Okay, sure.'

She smiles and from her shopping bag takes a paperback, a slab of chocolate, four apples. 'For you. And to read, a book by very famous Czech writer.'

'Monica, you didn't have to come all this way.' But he is very glad to see her.

She shakes her head. 'Don't be stupid.'

Nurse Dlamini comes in and switches on the television; he introduces Monica. She gives him a couple of pills and waits while he swallows them. Monica rests her hand on his thigh while they watch the news. He studies her profile: a strong jaw, a small bump on the bridge of her nose. He feels sleepy; probably the pills, he thinks.

When he wakes up Monica has left and the ward is dark. His elderly ward companion is snoring loudly. He switches on the bedside light. Half-past one. Next to his wristwatch on the side table is a note: 'See you tomorrow. Love M'

The old man rolls on to his side, mutters. He switches off the light. Soon the old man is snoring again. Somewhere outside the building a machine hums. Where is Louise? Does she really care so little?

MR MAUBANE: Mr du Toit, you state in your amnesty application that after you had enrolled at the University of Cape Town 'as it happened I met Mr André Pretorius, who had been at high school with me'. This is a bit vague. What was the exact nature of your relationship with Mr Pretorius?

MR DU TOIT: We had known each other at school, but had lost contact afterwards.

MR MAUBANE: Is it not so that he had been one of your best friends at school?

MR DU TOIT: He was a friend, yes.

MR MAUBANE: Did you know when you were in the Defence Force that he had joined the ECC?

MR DU TOIT: No.

MR MAUBANE: I find that strange. Would you not have had friends in common who would have informed you?

MR DU TOIT: I lost contact with most of my friends from school during my time in the Defence Force.

MR MAUBANE: And did Captain Harris or Colonel Visser not tell you this when they visited you in hospital?

MR DU TOIT: No.

MR MAUBANE: Mr du Toit, surely you realise that the following construction can be made, namely that Military Intelligence knew of your friendship with Mr Pretorius and for this reason you were selected to infiltrate the

ECC, as they realised you would have immediate access to a senior member of the ECC.

MR DU TOIT: I can see what you're getting at, but that's not what happened.

MR MAUBANE: You expect this Commission to believe that you had absolutely no knowledge of the activities of one of your best friends for four years?

MR DU TOIT: Yes, because that's how it was.

MR MAUBANE: If you say so. Let's then talk about the bombing. Who came up with the idea to plant a limpet mine in the hall?

MR DU TOIT: I cannot say it was any one individual's idea. We, that is Captain Harris and I, had on various occasions discussed various ways how we could disrupt those meetings. One of these ways was destroying one of the venues where meetings took place.

MR MAUBANE: But who made the recommendation to use this particular way?

MR DU TOIT: I cannot say. Captain Harris and I would have discussed the different options, and I assume Captain Harris put these to the chain of command, where the decision was made.

MR MAUBANE: Can you explain to the Commission who this chain of command was?

MR DU TOIT: I reported to Captain Harris. I have no knowledge of the chain of command above him.

MR MAUBANE: Mr du Toit, do you want us to believe that you did not know anyone else in the chain of command, that you blindly assumed that Captain Harris had approval from higher up for any command he gave you.

MR DU TOIT: That is how we were structured. In any case, a soldier is expected to obey orders from his superior officer. He is not expected to run around and find out from someone higher up whether his superior officer has the authority to issue that order. No army could operate like that.

MR MAUBANE: That's very convenient, isn't it? There you were, just a foot soldier, obeying orders, with no idea who your superior officers were, or who took the decision to bomb the hall.

MR DU TOIT: I don't know what you're insinuating, but that's how it was.

MR MAUBANE: Mr du Toit, please calm down. Let us now examine your version of the events on the day of the explosion. In your version, you did not meet with Tommy on that day.

MR DU TOIT: That is correct.

MR MAUBANE: According to the police report the limpet mine exploded at 20h22 that evening. And, according to your application, you were at your residence in Cape Town at that time?

MR DU TOIT: Yes.

MR MAUBANE: You also know that, according to the police report, a witness said that a few minutes before the explosion he saw a stationary car with two men inside about a hundred metres from the hall, in the same street. The witness remembered this because he was sure the men were white. Remember, this was during the State of Emergency, and white men in a Coloured township at that time of evening were very unusual. He thought it was an unmarked police car, as the only Whites they saw in the townships during that time were policemen ... (interruption)

MR VAN VUUREN: Mr Chairman, I can see where this is going. The witness was a ten-year-old boy, and at the time he was unable to describe the men or the car in any detail. The police report itself states that the evidence of this child was unreliable, and they decided that it was not relevant to the investigation. If Mr Maubane is in any way trying to imply that my client ...

MR MAUBANE: If I may. I was merely going to ask Mr du Toit if he had any knowledge of the identity of these white men.

MR VAN VUUREN: If in fact they existed.

MR DU TOIT: No, I don't know anything about that.

MR MAUBANE: Was there anyone with you at home that night?

MR DU TOIT: No, I was alone.

MR MAUBANE: Is there anyone who can vouch that you were at home at the time of the explosion?

MR DU TOIT: No, I lived alone in the garden cottage of a house in Rondebosch.

MR MAUBANE: Think carefully, Mr du Toit. This is very important.

MR DU TOIT: I am very sure.

MR MAUBANE: So you are unable to prove that you were in fact at home and not somewhere else?

MR DU TOIT: That is so.

MR MAUBANE: Mr du Toit, why do you think the mine detonated before the planned time?

MR DU TOIT: I don't know. I can only think that Tommy must have set it off accidentally, or that it malfunctioned.

MR MAUBANE: Please describe the remote control and how one operated it.

MR DU TOIT: It was about as large as a cigarette packet, perhaps slightly larger. There were two buttons, and a third, smaller one set into the mechanism. There was also a little instrument light. To detonate the mine the two larger buttons had to be simultaneously pushed for a few seconds until the light flashed red. Then the mechanism was armed. The third button had to be pressed with the point of a pen or something like that. Then the mine detonated.

MR MAUBANE: Surely then you must realise how improbable it sounds that Tommy could have accidentally set off the mechanism. The mechanism was obviously designed to prevent exactly that. Tommy would have had to accidentally press two buttons for a few seconds, and then accidentally push a pen against the third button. I think the probability of my winning the lottery is many times greater than that of someone accidentally detonating the limpet mine, don't you?

MR DU TOIT. Maybe, but people do win the lottery. It could be that Tommy was playing around with the mechanism. Or that there was something wrong with the mechanism, a loose circuit or something. I really don't know.

MR MAUBANE: And the only person who could tell us is missing. Mr du Toit, what happened to Tommy?

MR DU TOIT: I don't know.

MR MAUBANE: Isn't that convenient? So now everything can be blamed on Tommy. Let me put it this way, what do you think happened to Tommy?

MR DU TOIT: I can't say. He was a Cape Flats criminal with five thousand rand on him. Maybe he was robbed and killed. Or maybe he realised there was going to be trouble after the explosion and disappeared.

MR MAUBANE: Yes, Mr du Toit, all interesting possibilities. But the fact remains that his disappearance makes it possible for you and Captain Harris to blame him for the deaths of Mr Peters and Mr Pretorius, doesn't it?

MR DU TOIT: Is that a question?

MR MAUBANE: Mr du Toit, the fact is that to this day no trace has been found of Tommy. We weren't even able to establish whether Tommy ever existed as, according to Military Intelligence, all the records from before 1994 were destroyed. Tell me Mr du Toit, what do you think happened to Tommy, if indeed there was such a person?

MR DU TOIT: Well, obviously I know that he existed. But I think he's dead, no one can disappear for that long. But I disagree with you. From my point of view it is very inconvenient that Tommy disappeared as he is the one who can explain what happened that night, what went wrong.

MR MAUBANE: Chairperson, my assistant has just handed me a fax in connection with this matter that I want to read into the record.

MR VAN VUUREN: Mr Chairman, I object. If there is evidence that my learned colleague proposes to introduce, we must first have a chance to study it.

MR MAUBANE: I've only just been handed it myself.

CHAIRPERSON: Mr Maubane, do you have copies of the fax?

MR MAUBANE: I do.

CHAIRPERSON: Then I suggest we take a thirty-minute adjournment to give Mr van Vuuren and his client time to study the document. Thank you.

COMMITTEE ADJOURNS

21

It is an hour after breakfast. He and his mute companion – who, according to Nurse Dlamini, has not uttered a single word since he was found unconscious in a street a couple of days earlier – are watching a talk show. He feels better: the throbbing at the back of his head has mutated into a large bump; if he moves carefully his ribs don't hurt too badly. He is ready to leave but waits for Monica – she may supply his real address if questioned by the hospital staff should he be gone when she arrives.

Bored with the inane discussion on the television, he picks up the paperback that Monica brought him. He reads the publisher's blurb: a love story, it seems. But then he remembers: Louise had dragged him off one night to see the film adaptation. All he can now recall is the actress – a dark-haired and husky-voiced Frenchwoman.

He has been reading intently for half an hour when he suddenly realises someone is standing at the foot of his bed. It is Louise, silently watching him.

He lowers the book. 'Hallo.'

She steps closer. 'Are you all right?'

He forces a chuckle. 'It looks worse than it is.' He tries not to show how glad he is to see her.

'What happened?'

'Mugged by some guys on my way home.' He sees the doubt in her eyes.

She picks up his paperback. '*The Unbearable Lightness of Being*.' She raises an eyebrow. 'I'm impressed – since when do you read novels?'

'A present from a friend.' He reaches out to take her hand but she pulls away. 'I'm glad you came,' he says.

'I can't stay long. I have to get to work.'

'About the other night …'

She shrugs. 'Let's not talk about that. But I wanted to talk to you, anyway.' She glances at his ward companion.

'Don't worry, he's non compos mentis.' He smiles. 'And I doubt whether he understands Afrikaans.'

She hesitates, then speaks. 'I spoke to Dawid after I saw you the other night.'

He doesn't answer, but he guesses what's coming.

'I'm sorry to bring it up at a time like this, but I want to move on. If you don't sign the papers, I'll have to go back to South Africa to appear in court.'

He shuts his eyes.

'Please, Paul.'

'You're right, it's not a good time.'

'Why don't you want to sign? To punish me?'

'Louise, I want things to be the same as they were.'

Now she takes his hand. 'But things can never be the same again, surely you realise that. We've changed, you and I. I also made mistakes.'

She stops and her grip on his hand tightens. He waits. This is the closest she has come. The silence grows, and he hears the muted roar of the traffic in Fulham Road. Is it his imagination or has his ward companion cocked his head in their direction?

But Louise remains silent, so he speaks. 'I want to tell you why I didn't answer the phone that night.'

She shakes her head. 'Paul, you don't have to. It doesn't matter anymore.'

'No, I want to.' He takes a deep breath. 'The day before ... before what happened, when I met Tommy in Muizenberg, I saw that, even though I had explained a dozen times how to operate the remote control, he was still unsure how to use it.' Into his mind comes an image of Tommy, a bony man in his thirties with the emaciated features and shaking hands of a habitual Mandrax smoker.

'That night I couldn't sleep. I worried about Tommy, about him operating the detonator correctly. The next afternoon I broke all our rules and phoned Captain Harris, told him that we had to find Tommy and the detonator and complete the project ourselves. That's why we went out to Mitchells Plain that evening. We drove around the hall for a while, but we couldn't find Tommy. And that's when that boy saw us. We were still looking for Tommy when we heard the explosion.'

She looks sceptical. 'So why didn't you say this at the hearing? Surely it would have helped you? After all, you were trying to make sure that things would go according to plan, that nobody would be hurt.'

He shrugs. 'Do you think the TRC would have believed me? The two of us at the scene but blaming Tommy for what happened? Van Vuuren advised us to say nothing.'

She shakes her head. 'How many versions of the truth are there?'

'This is the truth.'

'Even if I believe you, it doesn't change anything.'

He decides to change tack. 'Why did you come here? To London, I mean?'

She blinks. 'I was offered a job by someone I met at that IT conference last year.'

'Who?' But then he realises. 'Adrian?'

She nods.

'You didn't leave because of what came out of the hearing, did you? You had this whole London thing planned before that.'

She looks down at her lap.

'Louise, what happened to us? I thought you, we, were reasonably happy.'

When she looks up her eyes are moist. 'Did you really think so? I don't think so. Weren't we just going through the motions? But I thought, I thought, you know, that things would be better once the baby … That's what I hoped.'

'But why didn't you talk to me?'

'Because we never talked anymore, not a real conversation, I mean.'

'What were you so unhappy about?'

'Please! Everything about that life. Johannesburg, the crime, South Africa, you drinking yourself into a stupor two or three times a week.'

He holds up his hand. 'Come on, we had good times too. And South Africa and crime, that wasn't my fault.'

She shrugs. 'I tried to talk about emigration, about Australia. A few times. But you didn't even want to listen. And …'

'Hang on, hang on! I didn't realise you were that serious. And I was sick and tired of everyone always talking about emigration, about running away, running away from our country.'

You see, there you go again.' She pulls her hand away.

'Are you serious? Do you really want to live in this country, this city?'

'Calm down. For one thing, it's safe here. I don't have to worry when I'm alone at home. Those nights you were out drinking I was always worried. Any strange sound and I would think, has someone come over the wall, is someone in the house?'

He snorts. 'Sure, it's safe here – look at me.'

She continues regardless. 'And over here I don't have to read every day how guilty I should feel about the past, for being white. I'm sick and tired of all that. I just want to live my life.'

'And Adrian?'

'What about Adrian?'

'You and Adrian – is it serious?'

'It's none of your business.'

'How long has it been going on?'

Just then Monica walks into the ward. Louise sees his glance, and turns around. Monica stops a yard or so from them.

'Louise, this is Monica, a friend of mine,' he says.

Louise gets to her feet, extends her hand stiffly. Both women look wary, and he sees Louise examining Monica. She is a head taller than Monica, and she holds herself even more erect than usual. The contrast between them is striking: light and dark, tall and short, confident and hesitant.

Monica looks at him. 'This is not good time?'

'No, no, stay,' he says.

'I was on my way, anyway,' Louise says. In Afrikaans she adds, 'I can see I'm in the way. You probably want to be alone with your *friend*.'

He hides his joy. 'You're welcome to stay.'

'No thanks.' Unexpectedly she leans down and kisses him on the cheek. He smells her perfume.

She turns to Monica. 'Bye, Monica. It was nice to meet you,' she says, not sounding very sincere. She takes a large envelope from her bag and puts it on the side table, next to his jug of water. 'I'll leave this with you then. You know where to find me.' On the flap of the envelope he sees the logo of Dawid's law firm.

Louise walks out of the ward without looking back.

'Your girlfriend from South Africa?' Monica asks.

'Ex-girlfriend.'

'She is very beautiful.' She adds, frowning, 'I don't think she likes me.'

'No, she's cross with me. But thanks for coming.'

'Mrs Sturgeon give me morning off. She also say you must get better.'

He sits up gingerly, dangles his legs over the side of the bed. 'I have to get out of here.' He tells her about the police visit of the previous day. His injuries are fine, he assures her. She keeps watch at the door while he dresses. On the back of his shirt is a large rust-coloured patch.

They walk down the fire escape to the ground floor. No one takes any notice of them as they walk through the foyer and out of the hospital.

22

He takes another two days sick leave. But he does not plan to stay at home. He has only one clue: the detective who came to take his statement had mentioned that Carl Makewell, the body-builder, worked as a nightclub bouncer in Camden Town. He will start there.

At first he can't recall the club's name, something to do with drugs. But then he remembers – Heroin. He searches the Internet, finds the club's website and jots down its address and closing time. He waits until his housemates are asleep before he leaves the house later than evening; it's better that they know nothing. He takes a night bus from Hammersmith. It's two in the morning when he gets off in Camden Town.

The night air is chilly. A couple of kilometres to the north is Louise's apartment; if he walked quickly he could be there in fifteen minutes. She is probably asleep. Maybe not, maybe Adrian is spending the night. He suppresses the thought; Carl Makewell is the objective tonight.

Heroin is on the High Street, and even at this late hour there is a short queue under the marquee. He walks on the opposite side of the street, the hood of his anorak pulled low over his forehead. There is a bouncer in a black turtle-neck sweater at the door, but when he gets closer he sees that it is not Carl.

He does not have to wait long. The bouncer is soon joined by another man whom he immediately recognises by his sloping shoulders and thick neck.

He watches from a doorway across the street. Carl obviously enjoys the role of gatekeeper: he barks self-importantly into his head mike and shunts the queuers back and forth. A few minutes after three the last clubbers leave and the doors are locked. Carl high-fives the other bouncer and walks away. His short gait is erratic, as if he's drunk or drugged.

Carl turns off the High Street, and then they are in the darker side streets. He keeps well back, but Carl never looks around. He could probably take him now, he thinks. For a few moments he considers doing exactly this, but decides against it: his side hurts and he hasn't planned the operation, a recipe for disaster.

After another kilometre Carl turns into a council estate and walks towards one of the two apartment blocks. He waits in the street, next to a row of cars. Carl reappears on the second floor and walks down the passageway. He unlocks the third door from the stairwell. He waits until Carl closes the door behind him before he goes into the estate. The lock on the door to the stairwell is broken, and the dark concrete foyer smells of urine. The doors of all the letter boxes are missing. He goes up to the first floor and examines the locks on a couple of doors – basic pin tumbler models, no problem.

The next morning he goes shopping: a pair of gardening gloves, half a dozen two-inch nails, a diving knife, a two-foot length of pipe, bicycle spokes, a hammer and file, pliers, a balaclava, a rawhide dog bone.

While he heats the point of a nail over the gas stove in the kitchen he remembers the classroom in the old whaling station on the Bluff. Towards the end of their year-long training they had been sent to Durban for a course in Urban Operations. One of the subjects was basic lock-picking, taught by an Army locksmith who showed them how identify various types of locks and how to make and use lock-picking tools. It was humid and dusty in the prefab classroom and from time to time one of them would nod off, only to be roused by a finger flick against the ear or a kick against a chair leg. But after a few hours they were all able to pick a standard lock in under five minutes.

When the point of nail is glowing red, he hammers it into the shape of a flat screwdriver and bends it eighty degrees. He again heats it, then dunks it in a bowl of cold water to harden it. His lock torque wrench is ready. Next he bends a bicycle spoke and files one end flat: a rudimentary lock pick. He cleans the traces of his work from the kitchen and discards his tools and surplus material in a skip in a neighbouring street. At four he packs a tog bag, carefully bandages his chest, and leaves for work.

Fergal Kennedy walks up to him in the kennels at Regal. 'Good to have you back. How do you feel?'

'Much better, thanks.'

Fergal insists on getting a full account of what happened, then asks, 'Any idea why you?'

'No idea.'

Fergal raises an eyebrow. 'Nothing to do with that other thing?'

He shakes his head.

'Good,' Fergal says. 'Have you had a chance to think about my proposal?'

He nods. 'I'd like to give it a go.' The work permit will be useful. Fergal need not know that he is not making a long-term commitment.

Fergal puts his hand on his shoulder. 'Good man. I'm off to Ireland tomorrow for ten days, but let's meet when I get back. I want to get the ball rolling ASAP.'

On duty it is a quiet night. Monica is away visiting her au pair friend in Surrey, and the hours drag by. He feels tense, jerky: pre-operation nerves. It is as if the last fifteen years never happened, as if the years at university and the tedious jobs have been erased, as if he's once more waiting for the signal to move in.

As for what he's going to do later tonight: right or wrong has nothing to do with it; it's a matter of survival, what needs to be done if he wants to stay in this city. There is some risk, there always is, but if all goes according to plan it will surely be impossible to connect him. A city of eight million people, one drug-dealing bouncer – it will hardly be a priority case. And his alibi is strong: he could not have been in Highgate and Camden Town at the same time.

At two he drives to Camden Town. He parks two blocks from the council estate. He pulls a hooded tracksuit top over his uniform, changes his boots for trainers. He glances at his watch; the club should be closing in twenty minutes or so.

Rex whines when he gets out. He takes his equipment and tools from the tog bag. He pulls on the gloves, lodges the knife and pipe into the back of his trousers, the balaclava into a pocket of his tracksuit top. The lock-picking tools he holds in his left hand. Finally he tosses the rawhide bone into the back of the van. Rex lies down and starts chewing on the bone.

Most of the flats, including Carl's, are dark, and the estate is quiet. He goes into the apartment block and up the stairwell. When he walks past the flat he glances down into the estate. It is deserted. He turns around and stops in front of the flat.

He slides the pick and torque wrench into the keyway of the lock, then slowly pulls the pick out to get a feel for the stiffness of the lock's springs. Next he applies pressure with the torque wrench, then slides the pick in again, careful not to touch the pins. Only now does he apply pressure to the pins and, as the pins set, increases the pressure, at the same time stroking the pins with the pick. After a minute the pick slides freely in and out of the key groove. He twists the torque wrench and the door clicks open. He pulls the balaclava over his head and pulls out the pipe. A pipe for a pipe, a fitting choice.

He slips into the flat, shutting the door gently. In the hallway he stands with his back to the wall and listens. The flat is quiet. After a while his eyes adjust to the half-light. He waits for a few minutes before he slowly moves forward. At the end of the hallway is a lounge with a television and a sofa. Immediately to his left is the kitchen, from which comes a sour smell. A passage runs at a right angle to the hallway. At the end of it is the bathroom.

There is one more door, on his left. He bends down and peers through the keyhole, then presses his ear against the door. He hears nothing. Slowly he turns the door handle; the door is not locked. A minute goes by, then another. He goes in fast and low, the pipe in his right hand. There is no one in the room. The double bed is unmade, clothes scattered on the floor. In a corner is a barbell, on the bedside table an assortment of weight-lifting and pornographic magazines.

Then he hears someone inserting a key into the front door. Carl is early. He steps into a cupboard and leaves the door slightly ajar. Adrenaline floods through him. He takes a deep breath to slow his breathing. After a few seconds the bedroom light goes on. He grips the pipe tightly. Through the chink he sees Carl walking past and sitting down on the bed. The bouncer grunts as he pulls off his shoes, then his shirt and trousers. He tenses his muscles; it is time.

But before he can move, Carl gets up and leaves the room. He hears the door of the bathroom shutting. A pipe wheezes as a tap is turned on, and he hears water running into the bath. His face is sweating under the balaclava. When the wheezing stops a few minutes later he steps out of the cupboard.

In front of the closed bathroom door he readies himself. He grips the pipe and makes sure the knife is lodged securely between his belt and pants. Then he janks open the door and rushes in. The bouncer is directly ahead of him, naked on the toilet, in his left hand a magazine and his right hand wrapped around his erection. Carl's eyes widen, and his arm goes up as he tries to rise. The pipe comes down hard on his raised forearm. The bouncer's yell is cut short by the thud of the pipe against the side of his head. He topples to one side and slides into the gap between the toilet and the pedestal of the wash basin, tries weakly to push himself upright and slumps back onto the tiled floor.

A strong bastard, he thinks, most people would have been out after that head blow. 'Get up,' he commands.

Carl struggles to his feet, his pizzle hanging limply. He switches the pipe to his left hand and boxes Carl's ear with his right fist. The bouncer staggers back against the wall.

Carl lifts his hands and shakes his head. 'Please.'

'Come.'

He keeps the tip of the knife against Carl's heavily muscled back as he marches him down the passage. 'What do you want?' Carl asks, and tries to turn around.

He hits him against the back of his head with the hilt of the knife and pushes him into the kitchen. He unplugs the kettle, cuts the cord and ties Carl's wrists together. The bouncer moans when he manhandles his injured forearm; blood drips from his head onto the kitchen floor. Then he leads him back to the bathroom. The bouncer brakes in the doorway and tries to back up. He punches him in the kidneys, and Carl drops to his knees.

His ribs aching, he drags him over to the bath. Carl is still winded when he pushes his head under the steaming water. The bouncer struggles furiously, but he holds his head down until the water turns pink.

He pulls him up and waits for the spluttering and retching to stop. It takes a while.

Carl starts crying. 'Why?'

He pulls off his balaclava.

Carl's eyes widen. 'Fuck, man, it wasn't my idea.'

He presses the tip of the knife against his throat. 'Tell me something quickly.'

'I'm sorry, very sorry, man.' Saliva and snot drip from his mouth and nose. 'I told Adam I didn't want any part of it.'

'But you were.'

'I'm sorry.'

'Who were the others?'

'Adam's mates, I don't know them.'

Again he pushes Carl's head into the water. This time he waits until Carl goes limp before he pulls him out. He touches his neck to ensure that his carteroid artery is still pumping. He sits down on the toilet and watches as Carl comes to and vomits water and half-digested bits of food on to the tiles.

'I hope your memory has improved,' he says when Carl is finished. Carl nods. 'I want to know everything about the others – names, addresses, where they work. Understand?'

Carl's memory is surprisingly good. For the next few minutes he asks questions and writes down the answers. When he is finished he folds the piece of paper and slips it into his trouser pocket. It is time, he has extracted all he needs. He feels calm, aloof; the thing in front of him is no longer human.

He grips the bouncer by his hair and pulls his head backwards over the rim of the bath, exposing his neck. With his other hand he picks up the knife from the washbasin.

The bouncer's eyes widen and he tries to pull his head away. 'No. Please.'

He puts the knife against the man's throat. But he cannot. With the slightest of movements he could, should, sever the jugular. But now he sees the face of a different man, a face he had forgotten, a man whose eyes had also widened in disbelief and terror, and he remembers the smell of the warm arterial blood that had pulsed over his hand in a dark bedroom in a suburb of Gabarone.

He lets go and Carl slides onto the floor. 'Thank you, thank you, man,' he says.

'What about Adam, the others?'

'We weren't going to come after you again, we were finished with you.'

He lifts Carl's bound hands behind his back. 'If you fuck with me again, or if I ever so much as see you again, even on the street ...'

Carl shakes his head. 'I'm history.'

He closes his hand around Carl's pinkie and bends it back. 'For your sake I hope so. And if you tell ...'

'Never, never.'

He yanks back the finger, feels the bone snap in his hand. When Carl stops screaming he bends down and cuts the electric cord. Carl rolls on his side and clutches his injured hand to his chest.

As he closes the front door behind him, the moaning dies away. He looks about – the estate is still. He glances at his watch: twenty-two minutes from start to finish.

Driving back through the quiet streets to Highgate he wonders about his hesitation. Why had he held back? A faint stirring of childhood religion – thou shall not kill, the sixth commandment of the Old Testament? But that history book too told a blood-stained tale, a tooth for a tooth, an eye for an eye, the wrath of a jealous God. And the legally sanctioned exceptions to the divine law are many: state execution, war, self defence. As for morality, that was self-delusion, a thin veneer of laws, customs and religious superstitions. The uniqueness of each human life? But fate, life, God, whatever name you chose, itself carelessly spent human lives. Genocides, massacres, famines, plagues – the death-roll was endless, whether you lived or died a matter of complete indifference to the universe. And once you grasped that there was no going back.

Squeamishness then, faint-heartedness perhaps? The first corpse he had ever seen was that of an enemy fighter whose skull had been shattered by a bullet, his face a bloody mushroom, his remaining eye dangling on a socket muscle. He had to turn away and swallow his vomit. But the more experienced operators casually dragged the body to a shallow ditch in which there were already three others. And in time a corpse had become a logistical problem, so much useless meat, rubbish to be disposed of, covered up, hidden away from the gaze of the living.

But perhaps there is something else, he thinks. A law of nature, like gravity, or magnetism, a law that holds that every action has consequences, that everything has a cost and that, although the account may come only much later, it is sure to arrive. Perhaps that is why he had held back, he thinks. But he is not convinced.

23

The persistent ringing of the phone in the kitchen wakes him. He glances at his watch: he has slept eight hours, a dreamless and unbroken sleep, the first in many months. After a minute or so the phone stops ringing. As he has to be at work only in two hours' time, he remains in bed.

He reflects on the previous night. The bouncer he won't see again, of that he is sure. Of course there are still the others, but maybe Carl had told the truth when he said that they were done with him. He'll have to wait and see, and from now on he'll be more alert. As a precautionary measure he'll move elsewhere. The timing is opportune: the new Regal branch will be in Ealing, he will find a place nearby.

It starts raining hard, fat drops that spatter against the window. The phone rings again. Other than Regal Security, Monica, Louise and his housemates, no one has his number. He goes on duty in an hour, so it won't be Regal or Monica. And a housemate he can ignore. That leaves Louise, but he has no desire to discuss the divorce papers.

He is in the kitchen when the phone rings again. This time he picks up the receiver.

'Yes,' he answers. The phone hisses in his ear, a long-distance call it seems.

For a second or two it is quiet, then a faint voice says, 'Paul, is that you?'

'Ma?' he asks, surprised.

'I've been trying to get hold of you all afternoon.' Her voice sounds anxious.

'Where did you get this number?'

'From Louise. She told her mother that she had seen you.' So they have been talking about him behind his back, he thinks. But before he can get angry she starts crying.

'Ma, what's wrong?'

'Your father's dead.'

A farm attack, he immediately thinks, breathing faster. In the last couple of years the attacks on farmers in Limpopo province have escalated, to the extent where there were now several murders every week. It is a low-grade civil war, and there were regular reports of torture, mutilation and rape of old and young alike.

But he is wrong. When his father didn't return for breakfast that morning, his mother says, she and two farmworkers went looking for him. They found him three kilometres from the farmstead, slumped behind the wheel of the Land Rover. The ambulance from Nylstroom got there only after two hours; according to the paramedics he had suffered a massive heart attack.

'Ma, I'm sorry.'

She resumes crying, then says, 'Come home, please. Pieter is flying back from New York tonight.'

'Yes, of course. I'll try to get on the next flight.'

Afterwards he sits at the kitchen table. At least the death was quick and painless – in South Africa these days one should be grateful for that. It is sure to be a big funeral: his father had been a well-known figure in the church and politics.

Strange, he feels nothing, he thinks, as he watches the rain trickle down the kitchen window. He should feel something, anything, but there is nothing, nothing other than irritation at having to return while he still has unfinished business here. He dials the airlines and gets a seat for the following evening; there's nothing available sooner, not even on standby.

He tells Monica later that evening when they are sitting in the van; it is still raining.

She takes his hand. 'How do you feel?'

'Okay. We didn't have a very good relationship.'

'But still, he was your father.'

'Yes.'

'When is the funeral?'

'On Saturday. I fly back tomorrow night.'

She turns towards him. 'Are you coming back?'

'I think so.' He suddenly realises that there will be matters – the running of the farm, what will become of his mother – that will surely involve him.

'I hope so.'

He senses that she expects him to say something more, but he remains silent. After a while she releases his hand.

'I better go back now.' She leans towards him and kisses him on the cheek. 'Have a good trip.'

He watches her walk away. There must be something good, something enduring to remember about his father. It seems he had spent the first twenty years of his life trying to please his father. In time he had realised that his father was only really interested in himself, his social standing, his political career. And then there was that evening in the Caprivi.

They had returned in the morning from a three-week operation – a joint SADF/UNITA ambush of an Angolan army convoy far across the border – to Fort Rev, their base on a barren patch of sand in Ovamboland. They were looking forward to a few days rest, but during their debriefing Captain Fourie informed them that that afternoon they were going to be flown to Fort Doppies, the training base in the eastern part of the Caprivi Strip. A delegation of high-ranking officers and politicians were on a border visit, and wanted to hear first-hand about their operation.

There was some muttering, but not much – Fort Doppies was a great improvement on Fort Rev. The training base was situated in dense bush between tall and lush trees and overlooked the grasslands and floodplains of the Cuando River. During the day herds of elephant, buffalo and lechwe grazed there and from the trees came the calls of swarms of blue waxbills, brown firefinches and swamp boubous.

When they landed at the base it was already dusk. Around a large fire in the boma about two dozen men were clustered, and there was the smell of meat being grilled. As he came closer he saw several generals and a cabinet minister, a much seen face on television with his Clark Gable moustache and eloquent rhetoric. Then someone called his name. Out of the group around the Minister came his father, his hand outstretched. He had not seen his father in over a year; on his last two passes he had travelled to Stellenbosch to visit Louise.

His father smiled at his surprise. 'Ja, I asked them to get you.' He had recently been appointed a member of a parliamentary Defence Force committee, he explained, and the purpose of their visit was to get a feel for conditions at grass level. He winked. 'I had to pull quite a few strings to get you here.'

'How are Ma and Pieter?' he asked.

But his father's eyes were on the group around the fire. 'We can talk later. Come, let me introduce you.'

The exuberant Minister, a bottle of beer in his left hand, shook his hand vigorously. 'Your father must be very proud of you, corporal.'

Next to him his father said, 'Yes, Minister. We du Toits have always been fighters. From even before the Boer War.'

He looked at his father, who as far as he knew had never worn a military uniform in his life. The Minister nodded approvingly. But then another civilian joined them and the Minister started talking to him.

His father led him around and introduced him to the other visitors. He watched how his father strutted and flattered, the intensity of his efforts correlated to the importance of whomever they were talking to. Afterwards they rejoined the cluster around the Minister. His father did not notice when he drifted away to the other members of his unit.

Later in the evening there were speeches, first by a general, then by the Minister, the usual rousing words: the total onslaught faced by the country, the need for vigilance against the Communist threat, the Defence Force's role as a shield while the necessary political changes took place.

The army chefs had taken great care with the meat, but the large trays of barbecued meat went untouched for most part - the sugar in the Coca-Cola mixed with the brandy and rum had by then blunted most appetites. He and his unit members watched the middle-aged officers and politicians getting drunk. From time to time he heard his father's voice rise from general hubbub. Twenty-four hours ago they had been in the field, skin itching from the black camouflage paint, unable in their ambush positions to rid themselves of the mopane flies that swarmed around them and the dust and aggressive ants that infiltrated everywhere.

Then a shot rang out. The Minister was pointing a 9-mm Beretta at the sky, his plump face shining in the light of the fire. He turned to the boma, eight feet in diameter, in which the large burning logs had by now transformed into a shimmering bed of white-hot coals. A general tried to restrain him, but the Minister shook himself free and leaped into the boma. Surprisingly nimble despite his large bulk, he dashed through the fire, emerging on the other side to loud cheering.

His father was hard on the Minister's heels. He made good progress, but when he tried to step over the foot-high retaining wall on the far side he lost his balance. For a moment it seemed that he would manage to regain his footing, but then he fell sideways. He put his arm out to break the fall, the palm of his hand pressing into the hot coals. His scream tore into the night.

The unit flew back to Fort Rev early the next morning. Before they left he went to the infirmary, but his father was still sleeping, his bandaged hand resting on his chest. When he saw his father a year later they did not talk about that evening. But he noticed that the skin on the palm of his father's left hand was a shiny pink

It is still dark when his shift ends in the morning. On his way back to Regal he drives past the Sturgeons' house. Monica is standing at the gate. He brakes, gets out. It has stopped raining and the air is crisp and fresh.

'Hi there, you're up early,' he says. She does not answer and, instead, steps forward, stands on tiptoe and hugs him. She holds him for ten, twenty seconds. When she releases him she turns around abruptly and walks back to the house. The cold air gives him the shivers. What are the chances he'll see her again?

He is busy packing his backpack when the doorbell rings in several short, insistent bursts. He looks down from Chris's bedroom window. It is Louise, briefcase in hand. The divorce papers, he suddenly remembers. She obviously knows about his father; ten to one she wants to ensure that he signs before he flies back. He goes down the stairs and opens the front door.

She is dressed formally: a dark trouser suit, high heels. 'Paul, I heard about your father. I'm sorry.'

'Come in, please.'

They sit at the kitchen table. 'Are you going back? For the funeral, I mean?' she asks. Under her eye liner he sees dark rings.

'Yes.' He looks at his watch. 'I have to be at Heathrow at five.'

'Sorry, I'll go then, I don't want to hold you up.'

'No, no, there's enough time. Can I make you a cup of tea?' She nods, and he stands up and starts to rinse two mugs in the basin.

'How do you feel?' she asks.

'Okay, I guess.' He turns around. 'And you, how are you?'

'Busy.'

'About those papers ...'

'Not now, Paul,' she interrupts. 'That's not why I'm here. I came because of your father.'

And suddenly he knows the time is right. He carries the mugs to the table, sits down. 'Every night I sit in my van, thinking about the past, us, André, everything. You know, the other day in the hospital, you asked me if I had told you the whole truth.'

She lifts her hand, closes her eyes for a few moments, then looks at him. 'Is there yet another version?' She shakes her head, pushes her mug away.

'No, wait, please.' He puts his hand over her wrist; she does not pull away. 'It was, is the truth. But why that meeting, that night? Did you never wonder?'

She frowns. 'You told the TRC you wanted to disrupt the ECC.'

He takes a deep breath. 'About Brad Friedman's affidavit at the hearing …'

She shakes her head, pushes her hair back. 'Don't. Please.'

'Louise, I knew about you and André. But Brad was wrong. André didn't tell me. I found out on my own.'

She looks down.

'It was in April of my first year at UCT. I dropped by André's flat in Tamboerskloof. That's when I saw you two on the balcony.'

She looks up, her face flushed. 'André and I, we …'

'Wait, I'm not finished yet.' He stands up and walks to the window, lights a cigarette, looks out at the backyard. 'I was angry, I wanted to do something.' He takes a deep pull. And then he surprises himself. 'I wanted to kill him.' And that is true, he realises. How could he have forgotten?'

Behind him she says, 'So it's true then?'

'No, wait. Not long after I floated the idea with Captain Harris that we should think about blowing up one of the ECC's meeting places. But by then I had calmed down. I just wanted to frighten him and his friends. I knew that André would be there that night. The rest was easy. Afterwards I convinced myself that it hadn't been my fault, that it had been an accident.'

When he turns around Louise is watching him; he cannot read her expression. He walks back to the table but remains standing. 'I thought you could get away from something like that if enough time went by, that it would go away. But it doesn't.'

She shifts in her chair. 'André … he started visiting me when I was a first-year student. At first nothing happened. It was difficult for me … I mean, you and I hardly ever saw each other, once every six months maybe. There were things, hostel dances, parties, functions. I needed a date, and he was there. And I was confused. You signed up for the Permanent Force. My life had to go on.'

Three, maybe four, years, and he hadn't suspected anything. 'Was it serious?' he asks.

She nods.

He feels tired, heavy.

They sit in silence. After a while she looks at her watch. 'I'd better go.'

He sighs. 'I'll sign the papers.'

She looks away. 'I don't know.'

'What do you mean?'

'I don't know anything anymore. Let's talk when you get back, that is if you come back.' She gets up. 'You're going to be late.'

They shake hands at the door. To a casual passer-by, he thinks, it will probably look like the conclusion of a business meeting: the suited woman with the briefcase taking leave of a prospective client, life insurance perhaps, something like that.

ON RESUMPTION:

MR VAN VUUREN: Mr Chairman, for the record, as I said to you during the adjournment, on behalf of my client I object to this document being allowed into evidence. The person making this affidavit is not here, and I cannot cross-examine him. We were also not told of this statement prior to the hearing.

CHAIRPERSON: Your objection is noted. This is not a court of law. This Commission is of the opinion that there are valid reasons for the late submission of this evidence, and that it may have a bearing on Mr du Toit's amnesty application. Mr Maubane, please continue.

MR MAUBANE: Chairperson, if I may then read the affidavit of Mr Bradley Friedman into the record?

CHAIRPERSON: Please proceed.

MR MAUBANE: 'I, Bradley Friedman, of 32 Allen Road, Toronto, Canada, do hereby solemnly swear that:
1. From January 1984 to November 1986 I was a student at the University of Cape Town (UCT). I left South Africa for Canada in November 1986. I am currently practising as a dentist in Toronto.
2. At UCT I was an organiser of the End Conscription Campaign (ECC).
3. Mr André Pretorius was a fellow member of the ECC organising committee at UCT.
4. Mr Pretorius introduced me to Mr Paul du Toit in February or March 1986. Mr du Toit was interested in getting involved in the ECC, and became an enthusiastic member. I never suspected that he was an agent of the South African Defence Force.

5. In about April 1986 at an ECC rally I met Ms Louise Smit, whom Mr du Toit introduced as his girlfriend, and who was a student at the University of Stellenbosch.

6. A few weeks later I encountered Mr Pretorius and Ms Smit in the Perseverance Tavern in Cape Town. From their behaviour it was apparent that there was a romantic relationship between them. Later in the evening Mr Pretorius confided to me that he suspected that Mr du Toit had found out about his relationship with Ms Smit, as Mr du Toit had recently become unfriendly and distant. He also said that he was considering telling Mr du Toit about the relationship, but that Ms Smit did not want him to do so. At the end of the evening he left me with the clear impression that he was going to meet with Mr du Toit, notwithstanding Ms Smit's objections.

7. On 2 September 1986, I was detained by the Security Police. I was released on 29 September 1986. After I was released from detention I met Mr Pretorius on one more occasion, but we did not again discuss the matter of Ms Smit. I cannot therefore state whether Mr Pretorius did in fact tell Mr du Toit of his relationship with Ms Smit. I left South Africa shortly thereafter, as I feared that I was again going to be detained by the Security Police.

8. I only recently found out about Mr du Toit's amnesty application, and of his involvement in the death of Mr Pretorius. I am not able to travel to South Africa due to work commitments, and therefore submit this affidavit, as I believe the facts as set out above are relevant to Mr du Toit's amnesty application.'

MR MAUBANE: Mr du Toit, are you still in contact with this Ms Smit?

MR DU TOIT (still under oath): Yes.

MR MAUBANE: What is the nature of your relationship?

MR DU TOIT: She is my wife.

MR MAUBANE: I see. Mr du Toit, were you aware of your wife's relationship with Mr Pretorius at the time you were students?

MR DU TOIT: I don't believe there was a relationship.

MR MAUBANE: Did Mr Pretorius not meet with you and tell you of his relationship with her?

MR DU TOIT: No.

MR MAUBANE: And your change in attitude towards Mr Pretorius?

MR DU TOIT: There was no change in my attitude towards Mr Pretorius. If Mr Friedman says so, he is a lair. Why does he not come here and tell these lies to my face?

MR MAUBANE: Mr du Toit, please stay calm. We are not discussing Mr Friedman here, but your attitude towards Mr Pretorius.

MR DU TOIT: Brad Friedman always had a big mouth. And where is he now, now that the new South Africa is here?

MR MAUBANE: Chairperson, can Mr du Toit please refrain from these outbursts?

CHAIRPERSON: Mr du Toit, this Commission will not tolerate this kind of behaviour.

MR MAUBANE: Mr du Toit, is it your contention then that

you had no knowledge of Ms Smit's relationship with Mr Pretorius?

MR MAUBANE: Mr du Toit, please answer the question.

MR DU TOIT: You have my answer.

MR MAUBANE: What is your answer?

MR DU TOIT: You have my answer.

MR VAN VUUREN: Mr Chairman, we have all heard Mr du Toit's answer that he did not know about this alleged relationship. My learned colleague is now hectoring the witness. The affidavit by Mr Friedman is not relevant to this hearing. We do not know what Mr Friedman's motives are in making these insinuations. The facts in his statement are unproven. How are we to know that Mr Pretorius in fact told Mr Friedman about a relationship, if indeed such a relationship existed? Or maybe Mr Pretorius was telling lies about his love life, as students are prone to do. Who knows?

CHAIRPERSON: Mr Maubane, the applicant has answered your question. Please proceed.

MR MAUBANE: Mr du Toit, is it not so that Military Intelligence monitored the movements and communications of the senior figures of the ECC?

MR DU TOIT: That may be. I had no direct knowledge of that.

MR MAUBANE: But you had indirect knowledge?

MR DU TOIT: In so far as most people in South Africa at that time knew that the State had opposition organisations under surveillance.

MR MAUBANE: Is it not so that you found out from the Military Intelligence structures that Mr Pretorius was having a relationship with your then girlfriend, now wife?

MR DU TOIT: That is very far-fetched, you are now chasing after ghosts.

MR MAUBANE: I must ask you once again to answer the questions put to you and not to make statements.

MR DU TOIT: No, I did not know about that, and I don't believe there was any such relationship.

MR MAUBANE: We can always ask your wife, can't we, Mr du Toit? I believe she is here today.

MR VAN VUUREN: Mr Chairman, my learned colleague is now being frivolous. He knows full well that she cannot be called without due process, and in any case cannot be obliged to testify in a matter involving her husband.

CHAIRPERSON: Mr Maubane, it is now half-past two. Two members of this committee have to leave shortly after four. Are you going to finish cross-examining Mr du Toit today? As you are well aware the hearing of Mr James Harris is scheduled to start first thing tomorrow morning.

SOUTH AFRICA

24

He wakes when the aircraft's cabin lights are switched on. He looks out of the porthole; on the horizon the sun is rising. The video map on the overhead monitor shows that the plane has crossed the South African border. His ribs ache and his knee is stiff. On his lap is the book Monica gave him in the hospital which he had finished during the night. It had evoked a strange response in him, for even though in the end the principal characters died in an accident it had felt like a happy ending.

He squeezes past the sleeping German tourist in the seat next to him, stretches his legs, then joins a queue for the toilets. When he gets back to his seat the monitor shows that they have just flown over Polokwane, a name he doesn't recognise. He examines the map, checks the town's location against Pretoria, then understands: Pietersburg – named after the Voortrekker leader Piet Joubert – has been re-named during his absence.

He looks out of the porthole again. Twenty thousand feet below, streams and springs sparkle in the morning sun, as if the flanks of the lead-coloured mountains are sweating. They are now flying over the Waterberg, so named by Boer big-game hunters in the nineteenth century. Halfway to the horizon the Crocodile River snakes around the southern tip of the mountain range. From one of its tributaries and two prominent peaks he triangulates the approximate position of the farm.

Half an hour later the plane makes a wide turn over Johannesburg, over chlorinated pools set like sapphires in the lush gardens of the northern suburbs, over gold mines dotting the ridges in the south, over a necklace of tin shanty towns encircling the city.

The black immigration officer stamps his passport, looks up, smiles. 'Welcome home, Mr du Toit.'

In the arrivals hall his brother waves at him from the waiting crowd. He walks towards him. Pieter's hair is shoulder length, a copper stud glints in his earlobe, he is tanned. 'Pieter!' he exclaims, surprised at how glad he is to see his brother.

They shake hands, hug awkwardly. 'Got in yesterday morning,' Pieter says. 'I told Ma I'd come and fetch you. Anyway, I was glad to get away from the farm.'

He stands back, slaps his brother on the shoulder. 'Afrikaans with an American accent. It's been too long since you last visited.'

Pieter smiles. 'Two years, not long enough.'

'And the tan? Sun bed or rubbed on?'

'Fuck off! Photo shoot in Martinique, for your information.'

They walk to Pieter's rental car. Sidelong he examines his brother. He has changed: he is more confident and at ease with himself. What a disappointment Pieter had been to his father: at school he had refused to take part in contact sports, and he had left the country after completing university to avoid conscription. But when conscription was abolished a few years later, he did not come back.

They head north on the R26 and Pieter tells him about his life in New York. They do not talk about their father. When the road joins the N1 outside Pretoria, he asks, 'And Ma, how's she?'

'I don't know,' Pieter sighs. 'She doesn't say much, and all the visitors are keeping her busy. It will probably hit her later.' Pieter turns his head towards him but his sunglasses hide his eyes. 'And you?'

'What about me?'

'How are you? I mean, after this whole thing with the TRC, and you and Louise …?'

'I've had my ups and downs.'

They drive in silence for a few minutes. But then, without knowing why, he says, 'Pieter, about André …'

Pieter glances at him, then back at the road. 'Paul, you don't have to explain, I understand.' In high school Pieter had sometimes trailed after André and him.

What does Pieter understand, he wonders. He continues: 'No, please listen. It was wrong what we did. I …'

Pieter interrupts. 'Ja, it was wrong to plant a bomb. But so was all that bullshit they fed us at school, all the stuff Pa was always going on about. And what happened was an accident.'

He looks at the houses of Pretoria's eastern suburbs rushing by. 'At the end of the day we are responsible for our choices.'

Pieter shakes his head. 'Those were fucked-up times.'

Thirty kilometres past Pretoria they reach the Springbok Flats, a landscape of undulating savannah grass with clumps of thorn trees. He remembers a story about something that happened here sometime in the nineteenth century: lions had killed the horses of two hunters one night and, a few weeks later, when a search party discovered the hunters' decomposing corpses they established from the tracks that the men had wandered for days in a ten-mile radius through the featureless veld, eventually dying from thirst at the campsite where they had started out from. He wonders how he knows the story, but he cannot remember.

Twenty kilometres from Warmbaths the southern foothills of the Waterberg come into view, shimmering and blurring in the heat haze. They stop for petrol and lunch in Naboomspruit. Inside the service station convenience shop a dozen or so people are queuing for lottery tickets. Outside, herds of carved giraffes, rhinos and antelopes line the pavement; on the forecourt, dusty cars and Hi-Ace taxis jostle for position. There is a large damp patch on the back of the petrol attendant's blue overall, and the hamburger bun is stale.

Eight cars and bakkies are parked in front of the farmstead. On the stoep he greets Tannie Marie, his mother's sister, and a couple from a nearby farm. A dozen people are clustered around his mother in the sitting room. They make way for him, curious faces turned towards him. He bends down to kiss his mother, then holds her; she feels small and brittle.

'Ma, I'm so sorry.'

She looks up. 'He went for a check-up only last month, the doctor said everything was fine.'

'Sometimes they miss things.'

She shakes her head. 'No, it was this other thing, this land claim thing that caused it.'

'What land claim thing?'

She inclines her head towards the group on the other side of the sitting room. 'Peet is handling it, he can tell you.' He recognises the sturdy back and neck of Peet van Zyl, his father's lawyer from Warmbaths.

His mother gets up and takes him by the hand. 'But come, get something to eat and drink, you must be hungry.' They walk over to the dining room table. 'The funeral is tomorrow afternoon,' she says, pouring the coffee.

He nods. 'Yes, Pieter told me.'

They are joined at the table by two women. When they start talking to his mother he goes back into the sitting room and taps the lawyer on the shoulder.

They go out on the stoep. 'Yes, the whole thing weighed heavily on your father,' Peet says. He explains: a year earlier the Bakwena Ba Magopa tribe had lodged a claim on his father's and two adjoining farms. They alleged they had been forcibly removed from the land in the 1920s and demanded the restitution of the land in terms of the new Land Rights Act. The Land Commissioner had ruled that there was a prima facie case for the land to be expropriated; the matter was going to the Land Court.

'But this makes no sense,' he says, 'I thought land claims had to be lodged by the end of 1998. And I remember my father saying at the time that he had checked, and that there were no claims. So where do they come from all of a sudden?'

Peet gives him a wry look. 'Department of Land Affairs is in a mess. According to the Land Commissioner this claim was misfiled – that's why your father wasn't notified earlier. And guess what, the date on the claim form is 30 December 1998 – one day before the cut-off date.'

'Sure. Can they prove it was lodged on that date?'

The lawyer shakes his head. 'You don't understand. They don't have to prove anything, the onus rests on the owner to prove otherwise. And the government pays for the lawyers for the tribe, so they'll fight you every step of the way.'

'But my grandfather bought the farm after the Depression, and then there was no one living here. It was bush, there was nothing here; he cleared the bush and started farming with cattle.'

'Doesn't matter when it was bought, how it looked then. It's up to the current owner to prove that the claimants, or their forefathers, did not live there, and if they did, that they left of their own volition.'

'But how you do prove something like that? We're talking about things that happened more than eighty years ago. Who's to say what happened? Are there records?'

Peet nods. 'You've hit the nail on the head. Of course not. And some believe that the government is behind all these new claims which are now suddenly popping up. They want the white farmers off the land.'

Peet lowers his voice and leans his head closer. 'Some also believe all these farm murders are part of this whole land thing.'

He nods but does not venture an opinion. There is no shortage of conspiracy theories in this country, and of those willing to propagate them. He waits for the lawyer to continue.

'But there are some weak legal points in the claim and your father was going to fight it. At the very least we could stall it for a year or two in the courts. And also, significant improvements have been made to the land since your grandfather bought it, which the government will have to pay compensation for. And the law does make provision for the government to give the claimants money, rather than land. So I'm reasonably confident that we will be able to reach some kind of compromise in the end. But now, obviously, it is for your mother, and you and your brother, to decide how to proceed.'

'What do you mean?'

'Well, the farm is in a trust, and you three are the beneficiaries.'

'A trust?'

Peet looks at him quizzically. 'Your father transferred the farm to a trust last December.'

After his hearing, after his visit, he realises.

It is after nine in the evening by the time the last visitor leaves. He sits on the stoep with his mother, Pieter, and Tannie Marie, who has been staying with his mother for the past two days. After his uncle's death, his aunt moved to a house in Naboomspruit, eighty kilometres away.

It is still oppressively hot. They talk about the funeral arrangements. Pieter and he will be pall-bearers, together with four political acquaintances of his father; the funeral oration will be made by an ex-deputy minister of the old government. A couple of hundred people are expected to attend.

Tannie Marie looks at his mother, then at him and Pieter. 'Pieter, Paul, your mother and I think it is better that she comes to live with me.' She takes his mother's hand. 'Permanently, I mean.'

He and Pieter are silent. In truth, he is relieved his aunt has broached the subject; on the way from the airport Pieter and he had avoided talking about the future. But what about the farm, he wonders.

His mother now speaks. 'Pieter and I have been talking.' He glances at Pieter, who looks straight ahead. 'Has Peet told you about the trust?'

He nods.

'And did he tell you that your father stipulated in the trust that he wanted you to take over the farm eventually?'

'No.'

'He thought it was best that you take over, he felt he was getting too old for all this. We wanted to retire to Somerset West. He was just waiting for you to come back from overseas to ask you to come and work with him on the farm, to take over in a year or so.'

They all look at him. Eventually Pieter laughs nervously. 'Obviously he wasn't going to ask me.' Their mother glances at Pieter, who shakes his head. 'Oh no, don't get me wrong, I don't mind, I'm quite happy where I am.'

'So what do you think?' his mother asks.

He yawns, stretches his arms behind him, decides to deflect the question. 'It's been a long day, I'm going to bed.'

25

The church is full. Above them three large electric fans stir the sluggish air. He and Pieter flank his mother; his aunt and other relatives take up the rest of the front pew. Behind them voices murmur and hymn sheets rustle. He was last here twelve years ago, for the wedding of a friend. Everything still seems the same: the raised pulpit with its carved woodwork, the polished pews, the large wooden cross suspended on the wall.

A door behind the pulpit opens and Dominee Viljoen, dressed in a black toga, walks in. All that remains of his once luxuriant hair are side burns and a grey laurel wreath, and he walks with a slight stoop. The organ sounds, everyone rises, they sing a psalm. He shares a hymn sheet with his mother and silently mouths the words. The voices behind him quaver; it is a congregation of old people.

Dominee Viljoen is not the fiery orator of old. He utters the expected platitudes – a beloved brother, pillar of the community and church, a great loss – without great conviction, and now and then wipes perspiration from a shining pate with a handkerchief. He tries his best to listen to the sermon, but his attention wanders. All he feels is boredom. But no, if he's honest, there something else too, something akin to relief, the feeling of a weight being lifted from him.

He glances at his mother; she sits with bowed head. Had their marriage been a happy one? It had been an old-fashioned union: his father made the important decisions, his mother ran the household. That was the way things were. And his mother had seemingly accepted that life, he never heard her complain. On politics she had not had much to say, other than to support his father. Even now he can't tell what she's feeling; she listens dry-eyed and impassively to the dominee.

And why did his father want him to take over the farm? Why had he put the farm into a trust? Did he have a premonition of sorts, a sense of foreboding? Now that he thinks back to his last visit to the farm, there had been a change in his father, a softening, maybe even a tentative attempt at rapprochement. But he had been too preoccupied with his own problems to notice. Or had his father felt sorry for him, the black sheep, unemployable in the new South Africa? Perhaps there had been an ulterior motive: at that time his father knew of the land claim. A poisoned chalice – had his father wanted him to help with contesting the land claim, to again do his fighting while he enjoyed retirement?

After the sermon a former deputy minister – responsible for Water Affairs in the dying days of the old government, according to his mother – steps up to the pulpit. He looks vaguely familiar, a florid-faced and overweight man who wheezes into the microphone. To think that that buffoon up there had been one of his leaders. And in the pews behind him is the old Pretoria elite: former senior civil servants, politicians, academics, businessmen, all securely in retirement now, beneficiaries of the high tide of Afrikanerdom. And their upright wives, probably sizing each other up even now, assessing their relative positions in the pecking order, thinking of how best to dish up the latest achievements of their adult children over the tea and sandwiches in the church hall afterwards.

The funeral procession winds its way past the holiday resort at the hot springs and through the town to the cemetery on the outskirts. The undertaker and his two black helpers wait at a discreet distance, shovels at the ready. The burial ceremony is surprisingly brief, a prayer and a psalm, then his father's coffin is winched into the ground.

Afterwards some of his father's acquaintances come up to him to shake his hand and offer their condolences. He can't get rid of the feeling that he is on a stage, acting a part; throughout the morning he has felt as if he is watching himself from a distance. And these people, these are his people, but he feels remote from them, repelled by them.

Late in the evening, after his mother and aunt have gone to bed, he and Pieter share a bottle of red wine on the stoep. They sit side by side in deckchairs a few feet from each other. The night air smells of wood smoke. Must be from the cooking fires in the workers' compound, he decides. He leans his head back, closes his eyes.

He is woken by Pieter's voice. 'Sorry, what was that?' he asks.

Pieter points to the firmament. 'This is what I miss in New York.'

In the dark he can only see the outline of Pieter's face. 'Do you think you'll ever come back permanently?'

Pieter waits a few minutes before he answers. 'I don't think so.'

'Why not?'

Pieter lights a cigarette. 'Do you really want to know?'

'Sure.' He takes the bottle from a side table and refills his glass.

'I like my job, I'm happy there. It's the centre of the advertising world.

And the Yanks don't care who or what you are – so long as you can do the job. As for South Africa, who knows how it's going to turn out?'

'What do you mean?'

Pieter shifts in his deckchair, turns towards him. 'Come on – you know. Do you really think things can carry on like this? Forty percent unemployment, a greedy and impatient black elite. Who do you think is going to get trampled in the middle? And already things are running down. Look at what we saw on the way here from the airport – potholes everywhere, cars and taxis that should be in a scrapyard, new squatter camps, cattle grazing next to the highway. And let's not forget about our president who believes in AIDS fairytales he finds on the Internet.'

'Growing pains.'

Pieter snorts. 'Sure, like the rest of Africa. Mark my words, anything that goes wrong in this country for the next century will be blamed on apartheid and the whites.'

He smiles. 'What happened to the liberal I knew?'

Pieter raises his hand. 'Hang on, he's still around. But maybe he's older and wiser. This is a black continent, a black country, and they have their own ways of doing things. Whites are sometimes tolerated, as long as they are of use or have money, and as long as they keep their mouths shut. Useful nuisances, in other words. But we mustn't forget that we're here on borrowed time.'

'Bullshit! You can't just wipe out the last three and a half centuries. We have as much right as anyone else to be here. And all the struggles of those before us, was all that for nothing?'

Pieter drains his glass. 'It doesn't matter what you or I, or for that matter any other white, thinks or says. The one thing that I can tell you is that the rest of the world wouldn't give a fuck if all the whites here are chucked out tomorrow. The South African movie is over, and the baddies should now disappear, like in a Hollywood film. As for our forefathers – don't make me laugh. Do you think they were that different to us? They did what they did for their own selfish reasons, for their own benefit, not for the generations to come. You owe them nothing. Whatever you do is not going to change the fact that they're six feet under.'

He is surprised: he has seldom seen Pieter express his opinions so forcefully. 'But don't you feel sad? Our history, our language, our land, all that effort for nothing.'

'Yes, I'm sad. But maybe it was never meant to be. Anyway, that we're here today is a quirk of history. Have you read the du Toit family history? I'm sure it's still in Pa's study.'

He vaguely remembers the book, published in the 1980s, around the time of three hundredth anniversary of the arrival in South Africa of the first du Toits, Huguenot wine farmers fleeing Catholic persecution in France. 'Yes, so what?'

'Well, at the time our ancestors came here, many more du Toits went to England and America. So our forefathers could just as easily have decided on America, and then we wouldn't be sitting here today.'

'If my aunt had balls she would be my uncle. And our forebears didn't go to America, and so here we are today. That's all I need to know of the du Toit family history.'

'You're missing the point. They came here from Europe, I choose to go to America, people move around, nothing is fixed. Why get stressed about it?'

They sip their wine in silence for a minute or two. Then Pieter says, 'Don't want to pry ... but any chance of Louise and you getting together again?'

'I don't know. Maybe.' Then, impulsively, he asks, 'And you, are you seeing someone, someone long-term?'

Next to him Pieter stiffens. He wonders if he's made a mistake, trod on forbidden ground. But then Pieter answers, his voice tight,'Yes, for two years now.'

'American?'

'No, he's Canadian.'

'That's good. I'm glad for you.'

They finish the bottle without talking again. Pieter squeezes his shoulder when he gets up to go to bed. 'Thanks, Paul.'

Something wakes him in the night; half-asleep he presses his watch – 04:20. He listens: a jackal is howling in the distance, the branches of the monkey thorn tree next to his room rustle in the wind. He is wide awake now, and he knows he won't fall sleep again.

He walks out onto the stoep, sits down in his father's horsehair armchair. He lights a cigarette. An unexpected recollection surfaces. It is something so surprising that for a moment he shrinks away, unsure whether his memory is playing true.

When he reached school-going age, he was sent to boarding school in Warmbaths as it was an hour's drive over dirt roads from the farm to the nearest school. But on Friday afternoons his father would fetch him for the weekend. On Thursday nights his excitement would mount, and on Friday mornings the hours dragged by. When at last the final bell rang he would rush through the corridors to the school gates. And outside, his bakkie parked in the street in front of the school, would be his father, talking to one of the other fathers. He would try and act grown-up and walk slowly towards him, but his father would lift him up and throw him over his shoulder and tickle him. And during the drive to the farm his father would tell him stories: anecdotes of the olden days in the Waterberg, tales of brave hunters and ferocious animals and, now he remembers, also the story of the hunters who had perished from thirst on the Springbok Flats. Back then his father would have been about thirty-five, thirty-six, and at that age he had already fathered children and was running a large farm. At the same age his son is a security guard, wifeless, childless.

He looks up. Millions of stars glitter coldly. Above him is the sword of Orion, on the northern horizon the Pleiades flicker in a hazy cloud of smaller stars, behind all the unfathomable depths of space. What a waste it had all been.

In him something starts to tear, and on his lips he tastes salt.

26

People wait three-deep behind the railings in Cape Town Airport's domestic arrivals hall. He scans their faces, then sees a petite young black woman with square-rimmed glasses, dressed in a cream trouser suit, holding up a piece of cardboard on which his surname is printed in large black letters. Miss (or Mrs, he's not sure) Motsepe, from the TRC's Cape Town office. She had been very helpful on the phone; the Commission encourages the perpetrators and the family members of the victims to meet. However, Mrs Peters had requested that someone from the TRC be present at their meeting and Ms Motsepe suggested that she pick him up at the airport.

A brief, tentative handshake, her hand cool and small in his; her name is Grace. They walk to her car, buffeted by the strong wind. They don't talk as she deftly manoeuvres her car out of the parking lot and the airport. After a kilometre or so the road joins the highway.

The squatter camps have spread since he was last here, a grey sea of zinc and wood and plastic that stretches to the horizon. The makeshift shelters have been erected on every available open space and cling to the sides of small hills, some no more than a dozen yards from the highway. These days they are called informal settlements, he remembers reading somewhere. You can keep your eyes on the road and the waves of cloud rolling over Table Mountain in the distance or you can look left and despair. All these people, he thinks, how do they survive, how do they endure, how long will they endure? Or does one in time get used to anything, everything?

He does not know where they are going as Ms Motsepe has not volunteered Mrs Peters' address, and is surprised to see they are heading towards the city centre; he had assumed Mrs Peters lived in one of the coloured suburbs on the Cape Flats, in the other direction.

They make an attempt at small talk which soon peters out. The car radio is tuned to KFM and they listen to the banter of the two disc jockeys. From time to time the car is shaken by gusts of wind. At Groote Schuur Hospital they turn towards the southern suburbs. A minute or so later they pass the campus of the University of Cape Town. Fourteen years ago – it seems longer. After André's death, he had become, somewhat to his own surprise, a diligent student. For the most part he hadn't mingled with the other students; on weekends he had driven out to Stellenbosch to visit Louise.

He ventures the question. 'So where are we going?'

Ms Motsepe keeps her eyes on the road. 'Tokai. Mrs Peters lives with her daughter.' He remembers the two young women with Mrs Peters at the hearing, but cannot recall their faces. 'How are you for time?' Ms Motsepe asks.

'My flight is at five o'clock.'

She nods. 'That should give us more than enough time.' She glances at him. 'Of course, it is up to Mrs Peters how long this goes on. That's how these things work.'

How exactly do these things work, he wants to ask, but refrains. There is a hollowness in his stomach, and he can't stop clenching and unclenching his fists.

At Wynberg they pass the turnoff to 2 Military Hospital. It is becoming a journey to his past, he thinks. But in South Africa the past is everywhere; it cannot be evaded. He had been heavily sedated when he was air-lifted here; for the first few days he was only vaguely aware of his surroundings. The bullet had broken his femur and shattered part of his kneecap, and the pain had been excruciating. It had taken four operations and eight weeks of rehabilitation exercises before he was able to hobble around without crutches.

The fence in front of Mrs Peters' daughter's house is a row of vibracrete sculptured hounds, lined up head to tail. On the unkempt lawn behind the fence is an inflated paddling pool, children's bicycles, a rusty barbecue, drooping roses.

He follows Ms Motsepe over the crazy paving to the front door. A curtain twitches in one of the windows. A jolly melody sounds somewhere in the house when she presses the bell. Behind the door he hears footsteps, then whispering. The door opens and a tall, slender woman with an angular face stands in front of them. Now remembers her: the daughter.

She greets Ms Motsepe with a curt handshake, avoids looking at him. Her name is Gadija. 'Please come in, my mother's in the lounge.'

Mrs Peters sits in an armchair in the corner of the crepuscular room. She does not get up when they come in. 'The light hurts my mother's eyes,' Gadija explains.

He and Ms Motsepe sit down on a leather sofa; Gadija stands next to her mother's chair. A shaft of sunlight falling through a parting in the heavy curtains separates him and Mrs Peters, and her face is in shadow. Underfoot is a thick-pile carpet, on the walls embroidered texts, in the corner a portable television.

Ms Motsepe begins. 'Thank you so much for agreeing to see us. I can wait outside or I can sit in, whatever you prefer.'

She addresses Mrs Peters, but Gadija answers. 'I think it's better that you stay.'

'All right then.' She turns to him. 'Mr du Toit.'

During the past two days he has rehearsed his opening many times, but now he does not know how to begin. His eyes are gradually adjusting to the gloom and through the drifting motes he sees Mrs Peters looking at him. Her face is impassive, her eyes dark.

Next to him Ms Motsepe coughs. 'Mr du Toit?'

He takes a deep breath, unclenches his fists. 'Mrs Peters, I never knew Ebrahim. I never wished him any harm. I don't have any children of my own, so I can't even begin to imagine what it must be like to lose one. I wish I could turn back the clock, that those things had never happened. I am sorry for the pain I have caused you and your family.'

There is silence, then Mrs Peters sighs. 'Why are you here, Mr du Toit?' Her voice is soft, restrained, but he detects something else, something harder. 'What else do you want from us?'

'Please call me Paul, Mrs Peters. I wanted to tell you in person that I'm sorry.'

Gadija snorts. 'You're sorry when you spill a cup of tea. I know why you're here. You think that if you come here and say you're sorry it will help you to get amnesty, don't you?'

Mrs Peters raises her hand. 'Please, Gadija.'

Ms Motsepe shifts in her chair. 'If I may say something?' She grimaces slightly. 'It is not a requirement of the Reconciliation Act that an applicant expresses remorse or asks forgiveness. So this meeting today does not have a bearing one way or the other on the outcome of Mr du Toit's amnesty application.'

Mrs Peters says, 'So, Mr du Toit, why do you think it necessary to tell me that you're sorry? Do you think it will make you sleep better at night?' She leans forward. 'As you said at the hearing, you were just doing your job, it was an accident. You're sorry, but you weren't responsible, is that not right? It was an accident, like a car running him down, or lighting striking him.'

He feels his heart beating, and the back of his shirt is sticky. 'Mrs Peters, please. I was wrong, we were wrong. It was wrong of us to fight like that. And I know Ebrahim would be alive today if it hadn't been for me. I am sorry, truly sorry.'

'Sure, sure,' Gadija says. 'You should be in jail, with the other murderers. You're only sorry that you were caught, sorry that ...'

'Gadija!' Mrs Peters interjects.

'Perhaps it's better that we go,' Ms Motsepe says.

Mrs Peters shakes her head. 'No, wait. Mr du Toit, let me tell you about Ebrahim, so that you know who he was. He was my first child, my only boy. It was a difficult birth, and for the first few years he was always sick. Twice I thought he wasn't going to make it. But at school he was always first in his class; even before he went to school he could read. My husband died when Ebrahim was fourteen and every day after school he worked in a shop to help out. When he was in Standard Nine, your police arrested him when he went with some friends to watch a protest march. When he got home three of his teeth had been knocked out, and his whole body was black and blue where they had beaten him. It was after that that he got involved in politics. He was a good boy. He was only nineteen when your bomb killed him.' She blinks, pulls a handkerchief from her sleeve, dabs her nose and eyes. Gadija kneels next to her and takes her hand.

He bows his head. Ms Motsepe shifts next to him on the sofa, and quietly rises. 'We should go.'

His shirt pulls away from the leather with a tearing sound when he stands up. Ms Motsepe steps forward, touches Mrs Peters' arm. 'Thank you.'

Mrs Peters look up at them, nods.

But when he gets to the doorway Mrs Peters speaks again. 'Mr du Toit.'

He turns around hopefully.

'I, we, just want to ...' She closes her eyes, then shakes her head, turns away. He waits for a few moments, but she does not look at him again.

Ms Motsepe takes him by the elbow. 'Come.'

They are silent until they reach the Blue Route highway. Then she says, 'It is not an easy thing for the families. They do not understand why there is no court case, why the perpetrators are still walking around free. It is difficult to explain this whole reconciliation thing to them.' She taps her indicator lever and overtakes a truck in the left lane.

He remains silent, waits for her to continue. But it seems she is finished. And suddenly he knows, and the realisation is overwhelming, that he cannot expect, does not deserve, anything.

He changes his booking to an earlier flight; at three he is back in Johannesburg. He drives to Pretoria. To find André's mother he does not need the TRC's assistance.

The frail care centre is on the outskirts of Pretoria's eastern suburbs. Outside the entrance of the face-brick building a bald old man and two grey-haired women sit on a wooden bench, their faces turned towards the sun.

He asks for her at the reception desk, then sits down on a chair next to a large potted plant. The floors are tiled, the reception counter marble or granite – it must get cold here in winter, he thinks. A few minutes later a stocky woman in a blue uniform comes down the corridor, and speaks to the receptionist. They look at him. The uniformed woman walks over to him. On her chest is a badge: Dorinda van Eeden – Superintendent. 'You're here to see Mrs Pretorius?' she asks.

He stands up. 'Yes.' Above her upper lip he sees the faint outline of a downy moustache.

She folds her arms across her chest. 'May I ask why?'

'I am, was, a friend of the family. I live in London at the moment, but I'm in South Africa for a couple of days, and thought I'd pay her a visit.'

'When last did you see Mrs Pretorius?'

'About fourteen years ago.'

She nods. 'Then I need to tell you about her condition.' She leads him into a small lounge next to the reception area. They sit down and she explains: André's mother was diagnosed with Alzheimer's disease a few years earlier; the condition is gradually worsening and she may not recognise him; even if she does, she might confuse him with someone else. He must not show any alarm at her memory lapses, or correct her if she repeats herself. But he is to introduce himself, preferably by mentioning something from the past – things that happened long ago she remembers well.

She leaves to fetch André's mother. While he waits he remembers something that happened when he was fourteen or fifteen. After school, it must have been in summer, he had cycled to André's house. He rang the bell several times, but no one answered. He walked back to his bicycle. But then he heard splashing from the swimming pool at the back of the house.

He walked to the side of the house and made his way through an overgrown passageway between the house and the fence. The gate at the end was locked. Shrubbery on the other side obscured his view, but through a gap he could see part of the swimming pool. He was about to call out when he saw André's mother swim to the side. She gripped the coping and pulled herself out. He shrank back: she was naked. But she had not seen him. She bent over, picked up a towel and started drying herself vigorously. It was the first time he had seen fully developed female breasts in the flesh. He watched, too afraid, too excited, to turn away. When she dried her back he saw a patch of dark hair between her legs. She wrapped the towel around her and walked out of sight. He ran back to his bicycle and raced away from the house.

But there is something else too, a memory so out of place on this day that he would prefer not to remember it, which is that for many months afterwards hers was the image that spurred his urgent masturbations.

Superintendent van Eeden returns a few minutes later with an old woman in a green robe. Could it be, he wonders, shocked. Her once dark hair is now grey, her eyes watery behind spectacles; she shuffles into the room.

He holds out his hand. 'Hallo, Tannie Lydia, it's me, Paul, André's friend from school.'

He sees the confusion in her eyes. Her hands fidget with the belt of her robe. 'Yes, yes, Paul, I remember. Where is André, is he coming?'

He looks at the superintendent but she does not offer any assistance. 'No, Tannie, he's not coming.' His mouth is suddenly dry.

Superintendent van Eeden says, 'I'll leave you two alone then.' She steers André's mother to an armchair, then turns to him. 'Ten minutes, that's all. She tires very quickly.'

He sits down in the armchair next to her. They are facing the windows and through the open shutters he sees the road that runs past the frail care centre, the sun glinting off passing cars. Across the road is the entrance to a scrapyard. He feels a weariness take hold of him. He sits forward, turns to her. 'And how is Tannie?'

'The people here are very good to me, I really can't complain.' She smiles. 'I remember you.' And it's true: in her eyes he sees a flicker of recognition. 'You and André were naughty boys. Always in trouble.' Her eyes sparkle, she chuckles, shakes her head. 'Boys.'

'Tannie, I'm here to talk about what happened to André.'

She looks alarmed. 'What's happened to André?' She leans forwards, clutches his wrist.

'Does Tannie not remember?'

She lets go of him, smiles coquettishly. 'Of course I remember you. You're the new doctor.' In her smiling face he recognises André's lop-sided grin.

He shuts his eyes. For the second time in as many days he feels himself slipping. Something has been stripped from him, a membrane of sorts, an excision that has left his nerve-endings exposed and raw.

He feels a hand cover his. 'What is wrong, why are you crying?' She strokes the back of his hand. 'There now, there now,' she soothes him.

MR MAUBANE (in argument): Thanks, Chairperson. I am nearly finished, let me wrap it up. Let's look at the objective facts. Paragraph (c) of Section 20 of the Promotion of National Unity and Reconciliation Act requires that Mr du Toit has to make full disclosure of all relevant facts. But only this afternoon do we find out that Mr du Toit was an explosives expert and that one of the victims, Mr Pretorius, was his childhood friend. He refuses to tell us what other acts he committed against the ECC while at university, and who reported to him. So I submit that Mr du Toit has not made full disclosure of all the relevant facts. Next, I want to examine the objective of the acts committed by Mr du Toit.

CHAIRPERSON: Please continue.

MR MAUBANE: Paragraph (b) of Section 20 requires us to consider whether Mr du Toit's acts were committed with a political objective in mind. Here there are several factors to bear in mind. First, in terms of sub-section 3(d), we must examine the proportionality of the act. The fact of the matter is that Mr du Toit was involved in the detonation of a highly lethal explosive device in a hall used for a peaceful meeting by a civilian organisation, which, on his own admission, had never committed any act of violence against the State. It is my argument and submission that the nature of the act and its probable consequences were completely disproportionate to the value of blowing a hole through the wall of a building with the objective of somehow intimidating the ECC.

My last, and most important, point is that sub-section 3(a) of Section 20 directs us to examine the motive of Mr du Toit. It is an objective fact that Mr du Toit was at the time in a relationship with Ms Smit, whom he subsequently married. But at the same time Ms Smit had also formed a relationship with Mr Pretorius. And, as we heard from Mr Friedman's affidavit, it is probable that Mr Pretorius told Mr du Toit about this. Even if he did not, it is probable that Mr du Toit found out about it through the State's surveillance of the ECC's senior figures. Mr du Toit therefore had a personal motive to harm Mr Pretorius. Once we know this, we also know how to explain the inconsistencies in Mr du Toit's testimony. That is why he can't remember who came up with the idea to detonate a mine in a hall used by civilians; he did. That is why he is unable to produce any witness to his being at home at the time of the explosion; he wasn't there. That is why a witness saw two white men in a car near the hall around the time of the explosion; it was Mr du Toit and, probably, his accomplice Mr Harris making sure that everything went according to plan. And that is why Tommy has disappeared; he never existed. And what was the objective of this whole exercise? To kill Mr Pretorius, and to so remove a rival for the affections of Ms Smit. The so-called political objective of destabilising the ECC was just a smokescreen. That is my submission.

CHAIRPERSON: Thank you, Mr Maubane. Mr van Vuuren, your reply?

MR VAN VUUREN (in reply): Very briefly, Mr Chairman, Mr du Toit's position as an undercover operative of Military Intelligence is common cause. It is also not in dispute that he was carrying out instructions from his superior officer at all times, instructions that he subjectively believed to be lawful. Also, it has not been disputed that the ECC had been identified by the State and the Defence Force as a threat to the security of the country. Whether this was in fact so is not relevant today; that was the view then.

As to the matters that are disputed. There has been

a statement that Mr du Toit has not disclosed all relevant facts. But that is a subjective statement. Why is it relevant that Mr Pretorius was a friend of Mr du Toit? In fact, in his application Mr du Toit discloses that he knew Mr Pretorius from high school. And yes, Mr du Toit was trained in demolitions, but, as has been said, no specialised training in explosives was required for this project.

Next, it was put forward that the act was disproportionate to the political objective pursued. That too is a subjective view. It was never the intention to kill or injure civilians, the intention was to physically destroy a meeting place of the ECC, with the objective of destabilising the ECC.

Then it was said that Mr du Toit committed the act with revenge in mind. This argument hinges on Mr du Toit's supposed jealousy over an alleged relationship that his girlfriend had with Mr Pretorius. But no factual evidence has been offered for the existence of such a relationship, other than the hearsay evidence of a person who is not present here today, and whose motives for only coming forward at this late stage are unclear.

And finally, this operation was approved by Mr du Toit's superiors, not by him. It exceeds the bounds of credibility to suggest that Mr du Toit somehow bamboozled the whole chain of command into this operation.

In conclusion, it is my respectful submission that the applicant has fulfilled the criteria of the Promotion of National Unity and Reconciliation Act, and that he fulfils all the criteria that are required and that he is entitled to amnesty.

I don't believe that there are any other matters that I need to address you on, Mr Chairman.

CHAIRPERSON: Thank you. That concludes your testimony Mr du Toit, you may stand down.

WITNESS EXCUSED

CHAIRPERSON: This committee will reconvene at nine tomorrow morning to consider the application of Mr James Harris. I thank you for your attendance.

COMMITTEE ADJOURNS

27

He is nearing the turn-off to Warmbaths when his rented cellphone rings. It is Captain Harris who, it transpires, got the number from his mother.

'I'm sorry to hear about your father,' Harris says. 'But why didn't you phone me to tell me you were back in the country? I never heard from you again after that day at van Vuuren's house.'

He is suddenly irritated: what business is it of his? 'Something came up, I had to go overseas.'

'I heard. Anyway, that's not why I'm phoning.' Harris laughs. 'We've made it, my boy, we've made it.'

He slows down. 'What do you mean?'

'Van Vuuren just phoned me. The TRC granted us amnesty yesterday.' When he saw Mrs Peters, when he was with André's mother, is his first thought. 'Paul, are you there, did you hear what I said?'

'Yes, yes. Let me just stop so I can talk.' He pulls over onto the concrete shoulder under a bridge. His hand trembles when he lights a cigarette. 'I'm listening.'

'Van Vuuren faxed the judgement to me. Let me read the end to you: "2. Paul Johannes du Toit is granted amnesty in respect of the explosion at the Mitchells Plain Youth Centre and the deaths of André Pretorius and Ebrahim Peters." Mine's the same. But it was a close shave. Judge Reddy gave a minority judgement that we shouldn't get amnesty.'

'Why?'

'The coolie reckons that we were lying about Tommy, that he never existed, that we detonated the bomb.' Harris chuckles. 'Tommy – may he rest in peace.'

A small muscle starts to twitch under his left eye. 'Jim, what happened to Tommy?' he asks.

'Come, come, don't make out now as if you didn't suspect.'

'Suspect what?'

'You know as well as I do that Tommy was a loose end, and loose ends are dangerous. But forget about Tommy, that's old history. We should meet for a little celebration, don't you think?'

He is unable to speak. He clenches the phone.

'Paul, are you there?'

He takes a deep breath. 'Jim, what else didn't I know?'

'You don't have to shout, I can hear you. You were on a need-to-know basis, and you didn't need to know. It was for your own protection. Same as the detonator.'

'What about the detonator?'

'Paul, I'm not going to talk about this on the phone. Let's meet.'

'What about the detonator?'

Harris sighs. 'For fuck's sake! You're like an old woman with a wet pantie.' He continues. 'Do you really think that we would have allowed a gangster like Tommy to run around with a live detonator?'

'Then who detonated the mine?'

Harris also raises his voice. 'Enough, enough. I phone you with good news and all you can …'

'Fuck you!' He hurls the phone onto the passenger seat.

For a few minutes he stares at the road while it sinks in, his rental car buffeted every now and then by the slipstream of trucks on their way north. The system of protective cut-offs had been watertight: Tommy, who thinks he is working for a right-wing organisation, plants the mine; he, in turn, is told that Tommy has a working detonator; someone else detonates the bomb; and Tommy is killed afterwards, or maybe even before. And that means it had been the plan all along to maim and kill the activists.

And who is he to complain about being used? The seed he planted had flowered well, very well.

The great project of three and half centuries: maybe once there had been something pure, something noble. But not at the end; at the end there had only been lies. He has been granted amnesty, and for that he should be grateful, but absolution he does not deserve, nor will he get it. The mark is on him, he will be a restless wanderer.

He drives on, takes the Warmbaths turn-off. The phone rings again, and on the display the same number appears as before. He switches off the phone. On the outskirts of Warmbaths he sees a new bar, an Irish-themed pub, part of a countrywide franchise. He turns off; he needs a drink.

Through the fog of smoke inside he sees a large group of men – local farmers, judging from their tanned faces and khaki shorts – clustered in front of a television set suspended from a wall. He orders a beer, turns to the screen. South Africa is playing Australia in the Rugby World Cup Sevens. He watches the game with little interest, and tries not to think.

After a while he becomes aware of a large blond man about his age glancing at him from time to time. His face seems vaguely familiar.

At half-time the man comes over, extends his hand. 'Paul, you probably don't remember me – Hein. I was sorry to hear about your father.'

Now he recognises behind the man's bronzed features a younger face, that of a skinny and quiet boy in the boarding school a kilometre or two from here. 'Hein. Of course I do.'

They talk during the second half of the game. Hein is married, has three children, and farms on the family farm; his parents have retired to the South Coast. The farm borders the Crocodile River, and he has oranges, paprika and lucerne under irrigation. In turn he discloses little: he is in the security business in London, he is married without children. Hein insists on buying him a drink. There are groans when the game ends: South Africa has lost.

He goes to the toilets. When he returns Hein is talking to three other men. Hein introduces them: Riaan is also a farmer, Ben the owner of a local garage, Charles a weekend visitor. They talk about the game for a few minutes.

Then Hein asks, 'What's going to happen to your father's place now?'

He sips from his bottle before he answers. 'I don't know.'

'Why don't you take over?' Hein asks.

He shrugs. 'What do I know about farming?'

Hein laughs. 'What do you have to know? It's a game farm, isn't it?'

'I work in London.'

'But that's no place for a white man.' Hein shakes his head. 'This is your land. We need guys like you.'

'What do you mean?'

'You know, with your military experience.' The other men regard him intently; they have been talking about him while he was away, he realises. 'We need more guys for the commando. Every week there's an attack somewhere, and they always go for the old people. I heard about your land claim.' He shakes his head. 'You won't find a buyer with that hanging over the farm. And if there's no one there, squatters will soon move onto the land, and with the new laws you can't get them off again. And that makes it more dangerous for everyone in the area.'

The other men nod in agreement. He doesn't answer and the conversation moves to the impending change of name of the town. Warmbaths is to be renamed Bela-Bela, Sotho for 'bubble-bubble'.

'They are trying to erase us from history,' says Ben. 'This fucking government has money to waste on changing names, but they can't even fix the roads.'

He listens to them venting their spleen. What did they expect? That everything would stay the same as before? Priorities have changed, a new herd of voting cattle has to be grazed. And if he took over the farm, what would the future be? Ferrying around rich foreign hunters, their Afrikaner guide one of the sights; complaining in bars about the new South Africa; eventually marriage to one of the local divorcees? And everywhere would be signs of a way of life that was over, that could never be again. Suddenly he knows what he must do. The realisation has been a while in coming, but it arrives fully formed.

He finishes his beer, refuses another. When he takes leave of them he senses their reticence, a vague holding back in the handshakes. They do not know where he stands, and that makes him dangerous.

When he turns into the farm he takes the dirt road that goes past the farmstead. He drives to the far end of the farm and parks next to the boundary fence. He switches on his phone, but there is no signal. He climbs up to the summit of the ridge. Now he is on the highest point on the farm. On all sides a sea of green stretches out to the horizon. The phone's signal indicator flickers back into life. He sits down on a boulder. He notices several red ticks clinging to his trouser legs; when he touches them with the tip of his cigarette they shrivel and fall away.

And now he is ready. The signal is still weak, but on the on the third try he hears the phone ring at the other end. It will already be dark there; he hopes she will be the one to answer.

'Good afternoon,' he hears her answer.

'Hallo, it's me, Paul.'

'Paul! How are you?'

'Good, good.'

'Are you coming back?' Monica asks.

He looks out over the valley. The sun is low in the western sky; to the east the bush is already in shade.

'Yes, I'm coming back.'

Acknowledgements

Thank you to Emily Woodhead for pointing me in the right direction. My gratitude to the staff of the MA Writing Programme at Middlesex University, London: Sue Gee and Linda Leatherbarrow for their support, Ferdinand Dennis for his invaluable help with the opening chapters.

And my enduring thanks to Annari van der Merwe and Jeanne Hromnik of Umuzi for their enthusiasm and editing.

Among the sources I used in writing this work of fiction are:

Truth and Reconciliation Commission: Various Transcripts of Amnesty Hearings and Decisions from 1996 to 2000 (HYPERLINK "http://www.doj.gov.za/amntrans/index.htm")

Stiff, Peter. *The Silent War: South African Recce Operations 1969-1994* (Alberton: Galago Publishing (Pty) Ltd, 1999)

Stiff, Peter. *Warfare by Other Means: South Africa in the 1980s and 1990s* (Alberton: Galago Publishing (Pty) Ltd, 2001)

Cock, Jacklyn and Laurie Nathan, (eds). *Society at War: the Militarisation of South Africa* (New York: St Martins Press, 1989)

The quotations from Arthur Miller's play *The Price* were sourced from Miller, Arthur. *Plays: Two* (London: Methuen, 1994)